A GIRL LIKE ME

A GIRL LIKE ME
AND OTHER STORIES

by

XI XI

with an afterword by Stephen C. Soong

A *RENDITIONS* Paperback

 ISBN 962-201-382-1

Renditions Paperbacks
are published by
The Research Centre for Translation,
The Chinese University of Hong Kong

General Editors
John Minford T.L. Tsim

Printed in Hong Kong by L. Rex Printing Co., Ltd.

Contents

A Girl Like Me

Translated by Rachel May
and Zhu Zhiyu

It really isn't right for a girl like me to have any love affairs. Which only makes it all the more surprising that such a strong attachment should have developed between Xia and me. I think it must be entirely the cruel hand of Fate that has landed me in this situation from which I cannot extricate myself. And I am powerless to fight against Fate. They say that when you really like a man, you can sit in a quiet corner just looking at him, and one little smile from him, even a very casual sort of smile, can make your spirit soar. That is exactly how I feel about Xia. So when he asks me—Do you like me?—I can tell him what I feel without holding back. You see, I am not a girl who knows how to protect herself, and the things I do and say are forever making me the laughing-stock of other people. You might think I look very happy when I am sitting with Xia in a café; but inside, my heart is heavy with silent grief. Inside I am really extremely unhappy, because of my premonition of where Fate is leading me. And I only have myself to blame. Right at the beginning, I never should have agreed to go with Xia to visit that school friend I hadn't seen for a long time; and then afterwards, I never should have accepted that first of many invitations to go to the cinema with him. Well, it's too late for regrets now. But the fact of the matter is that whether I do have regrets or not, I am no longer as worried as I was by the thought of our coming separation. Soon, everything will be over—for I have agreed to take Xia to the place where I work, and right now I am sitting in a corner of the café waiting for him.

I'd already left school long before the time when Xia and I started getting involved with each other; so when he asked me whether I had a job, I told him that I'd already been working for several years.

—So, what do you do?

He asked.

—Make-up. I make people up.

I answered.

—Oh, you do make-up.

He said.

—But your own face looks so beautifully natural.

He said.

He said he didn't like it when women wore make-up, he much preferred them to look natural. I don't think it was this conversation which drew his attention to the fact that I don't use make-up, but rather the uncommon paleness of my face. And of my hands. It was because of my work that my hands and face looked paler than those of other people.

I knew that Xia had got totally the wrong end of the stick about what sort of work I did, just like every friend I'd ever had always did. He must have imagined me at work, beautifying the faces of ordinary ladies, or embellishing brides in readiness for their wedding day; and he can only have felt even more certain that he was right when I told him that I had no regular holidays in my work, and that I was often busy on Sundays. After all, there are always so many brides on Sundays, or on holidays.

But making up brides is not what I do. What I do is to give a final embellishment to those who no longer have life; I make them up so that they will look peaceful and soft when they depart this world. In the old days I used to tell my friends exactly what I *did* do for a living; as soon as I thought they had jumped to the wrong conclusion, I would put them straight because I wanted to let them know what kind of person I was. But this honesty had cost me most of my friendships. It was me they were afraid of—as if I, sitting with them over a cup of coffee, was the embodiment of every dreadful spectre in their minds. I don't blame them for reacting like this—because after all, we are each of us born with a primitive fear of the mysterious and of the unknown. And so I had answered Xia without offering any explanation. There were two reasons for this: firstly, I didn't want him to be frightened—I felt that I would never be able to forgive myself if I ever again upset one of my friends by disclosing the macabre details of my employment; and secondly, I'd always been bad at putting things into words, and little by little I was getting used to keeping things to myself.

—But your own face looks so beautifully natural.

He said.

When Xia said this, I was acutely aware that it boded ill for our future together. And Xia?—he was perfectly happy, happy to be with a woman who didn't make herself up. His heart was light, but mine was heavy with sadness. I'm always wondering who in this world will do my make-up for me, at my end. Aunt Yifen? But Aunt Yifen and I are the same, and we both feel very strongly that we never want to do make-up for our nearest and dearest as long as we live.

I can't think why I carried on going around with Xia so much of the time, even after that bad omen cast its shadow. Perhaps I am only human after all, unable to control myself, marching left right, left right, in the footsteps of Fate. I really cannot come up with a rational explanation for anything I've done, and then I think to myself... well, isn't that only human nature, to be irrational? Much of human behaviour *is* inexplicable, even to the person who is acting in that way.

—Can I see where you work?

Xia asked.

—I can't see why not.

I said.

—Will anyone mind?

He asked.

—No, I don't suppose anyone will.

I said.

The reason why Xia wanted to come with me to work was

because I had to go there every Sunday morning, when *he* had nothing in particular to do. First he said he'd just like to accompany me there; but then he thought that since he would have gone all the way there anyway, why not go in and have a look around. He said he wanted to feel the excitement of the brides and bridesmaids, and he wanted to see how I made them as beautiful as roses, or how their natural beauty was spoilt by the make-up... whichever! I agreed without a moment's thought. I knew that Fate had brought me this far, to the starting-line, and that it was something I had to go through with. So, right now I am sitting in a small café, waiting for Xia to come; and then we shall go to the place where I work.

And when we get there, everything will become clear to him. Xia will realize that the fragrance he has taken all along to be a perfume that I wear especially for him, is actually nothing more than the smell of antiseptic which clings to my skin; he will also realize that the reason I always wear white clothes is not because I am deliberately trying to cultivate an air of innocence, but because these clothes afford me a measure of convenience in entering and leaving my place of work. The smell of that strange lotion not only clings to my skin, but must also have worked its way through to my bones by now—I tried everything I could think of to wash away that smell, but I never managed to get rid of it, and finally I gave up trying. I don't even notice it any more. Of course, Xia doesn't know anything about all this. He once said to me: What an unusual perfume you are wearing! Soon everything will be out in the open.

You know, I'm something of a hairdresser and I can do a stylish cut; and I am also an expert hand at doing up a tie. But where does it get me? Look at my hands. Just think of all the times they have trimmed the hair and beards of silent customers, and tied up ties around stiff and solemn necks. Could Xia stand it if this same pair of hands were to cut his hair, or knot his tie for him? These hands are really warm, but they seem icy cold to others. These hands should be quite at home cradling a new-born baby; but other people look at them as though they had turned into white bones, to hold and soothe skeletons.

There are perhaps many reasons why Aunt Yifen decided to pass on her skill to me. And from the kind of things she says, people would see it all very clearly: of course, with a skill such as this, a person really wouldn't *ever* have to worry about being out of a job, and the pay is pretty good too! How could a girl like me, with little formal schooling and a limited intellect, possibly hope to compete with others in this human jungle where the weak are the prey of the strong.

I think the reason why Aunt Yifen imparted the valuable secrets of her unique skill to *me* was purely and simply because I am her niece. She never allowed any visitors when she was working, and it was only after she took me on as her apprentice that she let me follow her around, learning from her little by little; and I didn't feel afraid, even when I was standing in front of those naked and cold corpses. And I even learned how to take the crushed or shattered bits and pieces of a human body, or the fragments of a fractured skull, and fit them together and sew them up, as though I were only a wardrobe mistress making up a costume.

I lost both my parents when I was a child, so I was brought up by Aunt Yifen. What has happened is that gradually, over the years, I have grown strangely like my aunt, and have even assimilated her reticence, her pale face and hands, and her slow way of walking. In every way I have grown more and more like her. Sometimes I can't help wondering who I really am—maybe I am a carbon copy; maybe the two of us are really one and the same person; maybe I am only an extension of my aunt.

—From now on, you won't need to worry about food or clothing.
Said Aunt Yifen.

—You also won't have to be dependent on someone else for your keep, like other women are.
She said.

Actually, I didn't know what she meant by this. I didn't see what was so special about learning her particular skill—surely there were plenty of other occupations that could provide for me just as well, where I wouldn't have to worry about food and clothes, and where I wouldn't have to depend upon someone else to support me, the way other women had to. But I was so very ignorant of the world, and definitely not equipped to compete with other women—and that's why Aunt Yifen thought to help me by passing on to me her special skill; she had only my best interests at heart. And if you think about it, what single person in this whole city can do without our help?—it doesn't make any difference whether he is rich or poor, a beggar or a king; when Fate delivers him into our hands, we shall be his last source of comfort, and we shall make him look peaceful and calm, and soft beyond compare. Aunt Yifen and I both have wishes of our own; but quite apart from these, there is one wish that we have in common, which is that never, as long as we live, do we want to do make-up for our nearest and dearest.

That's why I felt so sad last week. I'd already heard a little about this tragic thing that had happened, and then I discovered that it was my younger brother who was involved. As far as I understood the situation, my little brother had been in love with a girl who was not only attractive and nice-natured, but also very talented—they were so happy together that I thought they must be meant for each other. Despite all of this, however, their happiness proved to be very short-lived, and it was not long before I heard that she had got married to a man she didn't love, goodness only knows why. What sense does it make when two people who love each other cannot get married, but must instead spend the rest of their lives suffering, pining for each other. My little brother is a changed person, and not so long ago I heard him say: I might as well be dead!

I don't know what to think. Surely it's not possible that I shall have to make up my little brother?

—I might as well be dead!

My little brother said.

I simply don't understand why things have turned out like this, and neither does my little brother. Supposing she had said: I don't love you any more. Well, there wouldn't have been much my little brother could have done about it. But they do love each other, and it was not because anyone owed anyone a favour or needed the money that she married this other man. Surely in this day and age, there are not still young ladies who are being forced by their parents to marry against their will? Why should she have surrendered her whole life to Fate in this way? Ah, let us hope that we never have to do make-up for our nearest and dearest, as long as we live.

But who can look into the future? When Aunt Yifen informed me of her decision to teach me her highly unusual skill, she said to me: You must promise me one thing before I take you on as my apprentice. I couldn't think why Aunt Yifen was being so serious, but she carried on in a solemn voice: When my time comes, you must make me up all by yourself; don't let anyone else touch me. I didn't think it would be a difficult promise to keep, I only wondered why Aunt Yifen was being so insistent. I myself feel quite differently about it—for I can't see what difference it makes *what* happens to my body after I am gone. Still, it was the one hope that Aunt Yifen cherished above all others, and I felt that provided I was still alive when that day came, I must do whatever I could to ensure that her hope was realized. Aunt Yifen and I are the same as we make our long journey through life in that we don't have "great expectations"—Aunt Yifen's hope is that I shall be the person who does her make-up for her at her end; and mine is that I shall be able to put my skill towards creating a "sleeping beauty", a corpse more peaceful and calm and soft than all the others, just to make it seem as though death is really no more than the deepest and best of sleeps after all. Whether I ever actually manage to do this or not, it is only a game I play when I am feeling bored with life and I'm trying to kill time. And anyway, any effort I make is bound to be in vain... for isn't everything in the world devoid of meaning?

Supposing I ever *do* create my "sleeping beauty", can I hope to be rewarded?—the dead themselves know nothing, and none of their relatives ever realize just how much mental and physical energy I expend on my work; and I shall never be able to hold an exhibition and let the general public appreciate the quality and the innovative skill of my work as a make-up artist; and it is even less likely that anyone will ever write a review or a comparative study, or do research, or hold a seminar, in order to discuss the making up of the dead; and even if there *were* people who did this sort of thing, so what? Theirs would only be the buzzing of bees and the busy-ness of ants.

My work is nothing more than a game of solitaire I play in a small room.

Why then do I have my ambition if not to provide the incentive for carrying on with my work—because my work is, after all, solitary, and I am alone; and in the game I play there is no opponent and no audience, let alone the sound of applause. While I am working, I can hear only the sound of my own soft breathing; and even though the room is full of men and women, I am the only one breathing, softly. I can even hear my heart sighing and lamenting; and the sound of my own heart seems all the louder because the hearts of the dead are no longer uttering their sad cries.

Yesterday, I thought that I would make up a young couple who had committed suicide, who had died for love in fact. I stared at the face of the sleeping boy, and suddenly I felt that *here* was the raw material out of which I would fashion my "sleeping beauty". His eyes were shut, his lips were lightly closed; there was the trace of a scar on his left temple; he looked as though he was asleep, sleeping peacefully. Over the years I had made up faces by the thousands—many of these faces looked anxious, though by far the majority looked fierce. They were my standard repertoire, and I did the appropriate mending, sewing and patching, so that they would come to look infinitely soft. But the boy I saw yesterday, his face had an indescribable air of calm—had it been a real source of pleasure to him, killing himself? Anyhow, I knew that I for one wasn't taken in by his outward appearance, and I regarded what he had done as an act of extreme cowardice; and as far as I was concerned, a man who lacked the courage to fight against Fate was not even worth a second glance. Not only did I abandon the idea of turning this young man into my "sleeping beauty", but I refused to do any make-up on him altogether; I thought him and the girl so stupid for just dumbly accepting whatever it was Fate had in store for them, and so I passed the two of them on to Aunt Yifen, leaving her with the job of beautification, of carefully covering over the burns on their cheeks that had been caused by drinking a particularly lethal poison.

Everyone knows about what happened to Aunt Yifen, for there were people around at the time who saw for themselves. Aunt Yifen was still young in those days, and she liked to sing as she worked, and would talk to the dead lying before her as if they were her friends. Her reticence, you see, came later. Aunt Yifen used to pour out her heart to her sleeping friends—she never wrote a diary but she "talked" it instead; and those who were sleeping in front of her were the most wonderful listeners in the world because they could listen endlessly to every detail of her tireless talk. They were first-rate at keeping secrets too. Aunt Yifen would talk to them about the man she had got to know, and she would say how they were as happy together as lovers could be, but how from time to time they also had their cloudy days, which now seemed so far away. In those days, Aunt Yifen went to a school for beauticians once a week to learn the art of make-up. She went there regularly over the years, rain or shine, and mastered virtually every technique that the teachers there had to offer—even when the school told her that she had nothing more to learn, she still insisted that they try to think if there was not *some* new technique they could teach her. Her passion for make-up was so intense it was almost as if she had been born with it, and her friends thought that she was bound to open up some large beauty parlour. But she did not, and instead she dedicated the fruit of her studies to the sleeping bodies in front of her. Her young lover was ignorant of all this—he had always assumed it was part of their nature for girls to be preoccupied with their appearance, and he thought it was just that she liked make-up... that was all.

Until one day, when she took him to the place where she worked. And pointing to the dead bodies around them, she told him that hers was very lonely and dreary work, but that here there were at least no worldly cares, all conflicts over jealousy, hatred, fame or money ceasing to exist; and she told him that when people sank into the darkness, they would become peaceful and calm, and soft. He was so shocked, never having thought that a girl like her could be doing work like hers—he had loved her, he would have done anything for her, he had solemnly sworn that he would never leave her no matter what happened, and that they would remain devoted to each other for the rest of their lives, and that their love would always be true. Yet, before a silent gathering of dead bodies which could neither speak nor breathe, he completely lost the courage of his former convictions, and letting out a loud cry he turned round and dashed out, pushing all the doors open as he went. All along the way, people saw him running in blind panic.

Aunt Yifen didn't see him any more after that, but she was heard talking alone in the small room to her silent friends: Didn't he say he loved me? Didn't he say he would never leave me? Why was he suddenly so frightened? Gradually, Aunt Yifen became more and more reticent. Perhaps she had said all she had to say, or perhaps her silent friends had heard it all before and there was no need for her to say anything more—you know, there are some things which don't really need any elaborating. Aunt Yifen told me a lot about herself when she first started teaching me her remarkable skill. Of course, it was not the only reason why she chose me instead of my little brother, but it was the main reason... because I was not a coward.

—Are you afraid?

She asked.

—No, I'm not afraid.

I answered.

—Have you got a strong stomach?

She asked.

—Yes, I've got a strong stomach.

I answered.

It was because I was not afraid that Aunt Yifen chose me to follow in her footsteps. She had a premonition that my fate might mirror hers, though exactly why we have been becoming more and more like each other is something that neither of us could explain—perhaps to start with it was because we were neither of us afraid. We were completely fearless! When she told me her story, Aunt Yifen said: But I always maintain that in this world there must be people like us, who fear nothing. Aunt Yifen had not yet become totally withdrawn in those days, and she would let me stand beside her so that I could see how she put red on an unbending mouth and how she gently stroked an eye that had been wide open for so long, inviting it to rest. In those days, she still talked incessantly to her gathering of sleeping friends: And you, why are you frightened? How is it that a person who is in love can have no trust in that love but is a coward in love? Among her sleeping friends there were more than a few who were fearful and cowardly, and they were more reserved than the others. Aunt Yifen knew quite a bit about her friends and would sometimes tell me about them, like once when she was putting powder on a girl with a fringe she said: Gracious, how pathetic this girl is!—to have abandoned her sweetheart simply in order to play the fine-sounding role of the ''dutiful daughter''. Aunt Yifen knew that the girl over here had died in settlement of some obligation or other, and that the girl over there had died in mute acceptance of her fate—they had both surrendered themselves helplessly into the hands of Fate, as though they were not human beings made of flesh and blood, with human thoughts and feelings, but only pieces of merchandise.

—What an awful job.

One of my friends said.

—To put make-up on dead people! Ugh!

One of my friends said.

I was not afraid, but my friends were. They didn't like my eyes because my eyes were often fixed on the eyes of the dead; they didn't like my hands because my hands often touched the hands of the dead. At first it was just that they didn't *like* my eyes and hands, but gradually they came to fear them; and at first it was only my eyes and hands that they feared, but later it was my whole body. I have watched them leaving me one after another, like animals in the face of a raging fire, or farmers in the path of a plague of locusts. I asked them: Why are you so scared? *Someone's* got to do this kind of work—I'm good at my work, aren't I? And I'm qualified to do it, aren't I?

But gradually I became content with things the way they were; and I got used to my loneliness. There are always so many people looking for nice cushy jobs, and wanting everything to be all roses and stardust. But how can anyone test his strength and show his confidence when cushioned by star clouds and rose petals. I have few friends now, for they felt in my hands the coldness of that other fathomless world, and they saw in my eyes a myriad of drifting and silent spirits, and they were afraid; and even though my hands had warmth and my heart had fire, and my eyes could shed tears, my friends were blind to this. I began to resemble my aunt, having only the sleeping dead before me as my friends.

I wonder what made me tell them, when all around was a deathly hush: You know, tomorrow morning I'll be bringing a man called Xia to see you. Xia asked me whether you'd mind. I told him that you don't mind. Now, are you sure you don't mind? Xia will be coming here tomorrow, and I think I know how things will turn out in the end because my fate and Aunt Yifen's fate have already merged into one. I expect I shall see Xia struck with panic when he sets foot inside this place—gracious, we'll both scare each other out of our wits in our different ways! But I won't really be frightened by what happens—you see, there have been so many signs, I already know how it will all end. Xia once said: Your own face looks so beautifully natural. Yes, it is; beautiful to Xia. But even its natural beauty is powerless to dispel a man's fear.

I have thought of changing jobs; surely I am capable of doing the kind of work that other girls do? There's no way that I could be something like a teacher now, or a nurse, or a secretary, or an office-clerk; but couldn't I work in a shop, maybe sell bread in a bakery... or what about some kind of domestic work? A girl like me only needs three meals a day and a roof over her head—isn't there some way that I can fit in? Looking at it realistically, what I ought to be doing, with my particular skill, is making up brides—but I can't bear to even think about it. Imagine how I'd feel if I was putting lipstick onto a customer's lips, and suddenly they parted in a smile!—no, too many memories stand in the way of my ever doing the very work which suits me best. Suppose I *did* change jobs: would my hands and face ever lose their pallor? and that antiseptic which must have worked its way through to my bones by now, would its tell-tale smell ever completely disappear? and would I still keep it secret from Xia, my previous job, the kind of work I am doing now? It is disloyal to conceal the past from the one we love; and even though there are countless girls in the world all desperately trying to gloss over their lost virginity and their slipped-away years, I despise them for it.

I'm sure I *would* tell Xia that all this time I've been doing make-up for the sleeping dead. And he must know and come to accept that I am this kind of girl. So, it is not the smell of an unusual perfume that clings to me, but the odour of antiseptic lotion; and it is not because I am striving to cultivate an air of innocence that I am often dressed in white, but because I have to think of my own convenience, in entering and leaving my place of work.

But these are only insignificant details, like drops of water in the ocean.

When he knows that my hands often touch those sleeping dead bodies, will he still take hold of them—say, if we were jumping over a rushing stream? Will he still let me cut his hair, or do up his tie? Will he be able to tolerate my eyes gazing on his face? Will he lie down before me without any fear? I think he will be scared, very scared; and then after the initial shock, like those other friends of mine he will start to dislike me; and finally he will turn his face away altogether—all because of his fear. Aunt Yifen said: If it is love, what is there to be afraid of? But this thing, this so-called ''love''—though it may seem on the surface to be both strong and indestructible, I know that it is actually very frail and easily broken. A mask of courage is only a sugar-coating. Aunt Yifen said: Maybe Xia *isn't* a coward. It is the feeling that she could be right which partly accounts for why I haven't told him anything more about my job, the other reason being of course that I'm not one of those people who is good at putting things into words. Maybe it wouldn't come out right, maybe I would choose the wrong time and place altogether, or maybe the weather would be unfavourable—any of these factors might distort my meaning. To fail to enlighten Xia that my work did *not* consist of beautifying brides was in fact a test for him because I wanted the chance to observe his reaction when he finally sees the objects of my work—if he is scared, he is scared. If he immediately takes to his heels, then let me say to those sleeping friends of mine: It's as though nothing had happened.

—Can I see where you work?

He asked.

—I can't see why not.

I said.

So now I am sitting in a corner of the café, waiting for Xia. I've just caught myself wondering whether it isn't perhaps unfair of me to inflict this on Xia—after all, what's so wrong with it if he *is* frightened by the kind of work I do? Why should he be superhumanly brave? Why should there be any connection between a man's fear of the dead and his fear when it comes to love?—they might be two totally separate things.

My parents died when I was very small and I was brought up by my aunt—my little brother and I are orphans, we have no mother and father. I knew very little about my parents or what sort of lives they had led, and everything I *do* know was told me by Aunt Yifen later on. I remember her telling me about my father, how he too did make-up for the dead in the days before he got married. And that after he had decided he wanted to marry my mother, he once asked her: Are you afraid? And my mother answered: No, I am not afraid. I think it's because I take after my mother, and because her blood is flowing through my body, that I too am not afraid. Aunt Yifen said that my mother would live forever in her memory because of something she once said: It is love that makes me completely fearless. Perhaps this is why my mother will also live forever in the inmost recesses of *my* memory, even though I cannot remember the sound of her voice, or even what she looked like. But if my mother said that love made her fearless, I think that was only the way my mother felt, and it doesn't give me the right to expect everybody in the world to feel the same as her. I probably have only myself to blame, for having submitted to this fate, for having committed myself to such an unacceptable occupation. Who in this world *doesn't* go for girls who are soft and warm, and sweet as sugar?... and girls like that ought to be doing some pleasing form of work that is both graceful and ladylike. Not like *my* work, which is sombre and bleak, and cold as ice; and I think it has overshadowed my whole being with its dark cloud for such a long time.

So what makes a man as radiant as the sun strike up an acquaintance with such a gloomy sort of woman? If he were to lie beside her, wouldn't he find himself thinking of how her everyday companions were corpses?—and if her hands were to touch his skin, wouldn't the thought cross his mind, how often these same hands had caressed the flesh of the dead? Oh, it really isn't right for a girl like me to have love affairs with anyone at all. It all seems like a huge mistake, and I'm responsible—so why not leave this place and go back to work? I've never in my life known a man by the name of Xia; and, by and by, he will forget that he once knew a girl who did make-up for brides. But it's too late for all this, for through the window I can see him coming along the other side of the street. What is it that he's carrying in his hands? Why, what an enormous bunch of flowers! What big day is it today?—somebody's birthday? I watch Xia as he catches sight of me sitting in this dark, quiet corner, and walks over from the door of the café. There is bright sunshine outside; he has brought the sunlight in with him, for his white shirt is reflecting that brightness. He lives up to the meaning of his name—Xia, never-ending "summer".

—Hello. Happy Sunday!

He said.

—These flowers are for you.

He said.

He is obviously feeling happy, and he sits down to have a cup of coffee. We have had such happy times. But what is happiness after all—happiness is always quickly over. My heart is weighed down by so much sorrow. Only a short walk, no more than three hundred yards from here, and we'll be at my work-place. And then, just like what happened many years ago, a panic-stricken man will go dashing out through those large doors, and curious eyes will follow him until he completely disappears from sight. Aunt Yifen said that maybe there are still some courageous people left in this world who fear nothing. But I knew at the time that what she said was only conjecture, and I thought exactly the same thing again when I saw Xia walking along the other side of the street with an enormous bunch of flowers in his hands...because this was a bad omen. Oh, it really isn't right for a girl like me to have love affairs with anyone at all. Perhaps I should say to those sleeping friends of mine: Don't you think we're the same, you and I? Decades can flash past with the blink of an eye. It is totally unnecessary for anybody to be scared to death by anybody else, for no matter what reason. The enormous bunch of flowers Xia has brought into the café, they are so very beautiful; he is happy, whereas I am full of grief. He doesn't realize that in our line of business, flowers are a last goodbye.

The Cold

Translated by Hannah Cheung and John Minford

This cold of mine, I'll never get rid of it.

I thought.

In fact, the cold is incurable.

I thought.

I was thinking these thoughts, sitting on a rocking chair in my family doctor's house. My doctor did not know what I was thinking, which was why he went on interminably discussing various problems connected with the common cold. He was a very talkative man.

"Each one of us has a thermostat in the brain."

He said.

I nodded.

As a matter of fact, in our brains we all think things other people can never know, I thought.

"When the weather is cold, the thermostat makes us shiver, and our bodies generate heat."

He said.

I nodded.

When the weather is cold, my cold will get worse, I thought.

"When the weather is warm, the thermostat makes us perspire, and our body temperature drops rapidly."

He said.

I nodded.

When the weather is warm? It was warm when I caught my cold, I thought.

"But when a cold strikes, something unusual happens to disrupt the thermostatic system in our bodies, and our body temperature rises suddenly.''

He said.

I kept nodding at my doctor.

Well yes, when my cold struck me, something unusual did happen. And yet no, no it was because something unusual happened, that the cold struck, I thought.

Sitting on the rocking chair in my family doctor's house, I had not actually been listening to a word he was saying. I nodded at him every now and then, because he was speaking to me. I could hear him talking about thermostats, thermostatic systems, cold weather, warm weather, something striking, something unusual. Broken strands of speech drifted into my ears. I thought he must have suddenly started talking to me like this about fluctuations in temperature and the weather because he could see that I had a cold. I had wiped my nose with a tissue just as I came in. Then, during the considerable period I had been sitting there in his house, I had coughed several times. He shook his head at me as he had done in the past: ''Haven't you got rid of that cold of yours yet?''

My last meeting with our family doctor had been in his clinic. I had taken my mother there for a check-up. My mother had slightly high blood pressure and I used to take her to the clinic every other month. So I often met our family doctor. The last time I went to the clinic with my mother, I already had the cold, and there was no hiding it. So he said, ''Oh dear, Little Fish, how come you've caught a cold?'' Every time I had some slight illness, he would speak to me like that; he would always say ''Oh dear, Little Fish, how come you've...''

My doctor never called me by my name, he never addressed me as Miss Yu; he always called me Little Fish, because that was what all my family called me. Little Fish was the nickname my relatives had given me when I was small. My doctor watched me grow up, just as my father did; it was he who delivered me into the world. This doctor who called me Little Fish had an excellent memory. He always knew the medical history of every member of our family, down to the last detail. He would even remember what precise ailment we had been suffering from on our last visit. He must have remembered that I had a cold when I had last gone to his clinic. That was why he said: "Haven't you got rid of that cold of yours yet?"

This time I had visited my doctor's place on my own, and not for a consultation. That was why I had gone to his house, and not his clinic. But he was still so concerned about my health that he went into his bedroom and came out shortly afterwards with a small paper bag for me, full of pills of various colours.

"You must drink more water."

He told me.

I nodded.

"You must get out in the sun more."

He told me.

I nodded.

"Try to rest more."

He told me.

I nodded again.

This time I was really listening, I was really nodding in response. But what was the use now, even if he was so concerned about my health and had given me such careful instructions? I only knew the fact, which was that my cold was incurable.

I had gone to my doctor's house this time not to ask him for a cold remedy, but to deliver an invitation card to my wedding, and to ask him to come to the ceremony, no matter how busy he might be.

"Hid! Hid!" the fish-hawk saith,
by isle in Ho the fish-hawk saith:
"Dark and clear,
Dark and clear,
So shall be the prince's fere."

"So it's the bride."

He said, opening the invitation.

I think my face must have looked pale.

"You have kept me waiting for this so long."

He said, handing me a glass of lemon-juice.

I think my hand quivered slightly.

"Certainly I will come, most certainly."

He said, patting my head gently.

I think I felt a bit dizzy.

When I left, I asked him again to be sure to be at my wedding, come what may. He said again he would certainly come, and then I bade him farewell. He must have noticed my pale face and my forlorn expression, and he patted me on the shoulder again and said: "Go home and get some rest. You're going to be a bride soon." He must have thought my low spirits were caused by my cold; how could he know the truth, that they stemmed from something else, from a deep sorrow. I bade him farewell and went on to other places where I had to deliver more invitations. I was carrying a small brown paper envelope with a few invitation cards inside it. Only a few, but they felt so heavy. Ah, after the autumn I would have to get married.

O omen tree, that art so frail and young,
so glossy fair to shine with flaming flower;
that goest to wed
and make fair house and bower.

After the autumn, I would have to get married.

O peach-tree thou art fair
as leaf amid new boughs;
going to bride;
to build thy man his house.

It was almost a year since I had been engaged. We had been engaged all this time, and our parents felt we should get married. Before our engagement, my fiancé and I had known each other slightly. My father and his father had business connections and both loved tennis, so we often saw each other at the tennis-courts. I never formed any particular impression of my fiancé, I just thought him a respectable and upright kind of person, with a good job and a steady way of life. Except when he was in his casual sports-clothes, he was always more smartly dressed than other people, and he usually wore a tie.

In fact, I knew little about my fiancé. Although we often met at the tennis-courts, we only exchanged greetings like "Good morning", "How are you", or he might ask me what I wanted to drink and move my chair for me. I thought he probably listened to classical music in his spare time, because once when I said I rather liked Schubert, he said he liked the Trout Quintet best. Perhaps because I enjoy classical music, later on we occasionally went to concerts together.

We were engaged last year, by which time I was already thirty-two. Of course I had left school long before then.

After leaving school, I had no trouble finding a job I liked, and in this way I had worked—44 hours per week—for seven or eight years. During all that time, my life had been a quiet and lonely one, for I was not a sociable person and I had no particularly intimate friends. Not that I was a totally friendless person. I made some friends at school, but after seven or eight years they had either got married, gone away, or we had somehow lost contact. I still met one or two of them occasionally, but we each had our work to do and seldom got together.

I was already thirty-two when I became engaged. Possibly I became engaged because my parents suddenly realised that I was already thirty-two.

The days and months hurried on, never delaying;
Springs and autumns sped by in endless alternation.

My parents could not have discovered the fact that I was already thirty-two all of a sudden. They must have watched me grow and change quietly from when I was twenty-two. They must have counted the years for me one by one: twenty-three, twenty-four, twenty-five, and then twenty-eight, twenty-nine, thirty. When they got to thirty, they must have begun to worry—why does our daughter show no sign of having a young man? That must have been why they gazed at me so often. All along I had been getting on fine at home; I went to work on time, came back from work on time, occasionally I went out to lunch with a colleague. On holidays I would go swimming with my younger brother. If father played tennis, we would go to the tennis-courts with him. It was a quiet life and it suited me very well. But it worried my parents that I was so quiet.

Even on Saturday evenings I would often just stay in my little room alone and listen to music, or read. Sometimes I had thought it might be nice to have a close friend, someone who could really share my interests. We could go out for a cup of coffee and a nice chat. But I had no such friend. At school there had been so many friends in class; it was fun, we talked freely about everything under the sun. Some of my classmates were quite brilliant. Like Chu.

My parents often sat in the sitting-room after dinner to watch television. In fact, they seldom really watched television, they just sat there for a rest. And often they started talking about me and went on at great length. Sometimes I heard them, sometimes I didn't. After a long time, little by little, I began to piece together their meaning. Their conversations gradually took on a shape, they seemed to be parts of one continuous dialogue.

"Not a single friend?"

My father said.

A face drifted before my eyes.

"Apparently not."

My mother said.

He often wore white.

"It's been like this for years now,"

My father said.

Such white clothes.

Blue, blue collar, my heart's delight...

"I know she hasn't."

My mother said.

Corduroy trousers.

Blue, blue sash, my heart's misery.

"Doesn't she go swimming quite a lot?"

My father said.
Sandals.
"With her younger brother."
My mother said.
A lovely smile.
...my clear eyed man.
"And she goes to the movies as well."
My father said.
His name was Chu.
"But always alone."
My mother said.
Wonder how he is now.
"No one ever calls her up."
My father said.
Why was I thinking about him...
"And no visitors either."
My mother said.
But he had never paid me any attention.
"Thirty-two already."
My father said.
Perhaps he already has a family of his own.
I am gathering wild figs in the water!
I am looking for lotuses in the tree-tops!
"What do you think?"
My mother asked.

My parents made the arrangements, and I was finally engaged. I don't know what I said when my mother asked me what I thought about it. Probably nothing. What could I say? I just felt that my parents did not want me any more. If only I could have spent my life peacefully at my home. (Was it mine?) It was such a melancholy time. When a girl grows up at home, grows old at home, her parents feel uneasy, they feel as if they are losing face. So I thought I ought to do this for them. I got engaged out of this desultory, helpless feeling. In fact I had no choice. I had no close friend, no one who shared my interests and thoughts. What kind of man could I choose for a husband? My fiancé was a nice enough man. We were not totally unfamiliar with each other. He was polite and considerate to me; he carried my sports-clothes for me after tennis, he bought concert tickets specially for me. I was already thirty-two. What other choice did I still have? Was I to spend my whole life in my parents' house and let them go on counting for me—thirty-six, thirty-seven, thirty-eight... forty-five, forty-six, forty-seven?

"Oh, Miss Fish, you must have caught a cold."

Old Mrs Chu said.

"No, no."

Though I repeatedly denied it, I still sneezed—twice.

"Look at you! And you still try to deny it. Didn't you just sneeze?"

Old Mrs Chu said.

"The air-conditioning is rather too cold."

I said.

It was rather cold in the café. I had come in a hurry and left my thin woollen cardigan in my office. It was a Saturday morning in summer. Almost noontime. I was still working in the Social Welfare Department, and recently had been interviewing elderly people in my small office. They came to collect their old-age pensions. Of course, they did not have to come and collect the money every month from our office. It was transferred direct into their bank accounts. But still we asked them to come once a year so that we could meet them, and know they were still alive. Over the past few days, old people had been appearing in our office in droves from morning till evening.

Several weeks before, we had sent letters out to the pensioners in the neighbourhood, and they came in batches, most of them with a member of their family. Some walked, some came by taxi. Some were escorted by one or even two relatives, while the more robust among them came on their own. Most of the escorts were women, and as a result it was very noisy in the lobby, with the pensioners and their escorts sitting in pairs and chattering away endlessly.

There were several long benches in the lobby, and the

pensioners who had come for interview all sat waiting on the benches. It was Saturday, it was so fine outside, a beautiful summer's day. Since it was Saturday, I was in a particularly relaxed mood. In less than an hour's time I would be off work. On Saturday afternoons in summer whenever it was fine, I always went swimming with my younger brother. He and I both enjoyed swimming, while my father stuck to tennis.

I looked at my watch. It was a quarter to one. There was still one pensioner to interview, and I could go home. And after lunch I could go swimming with my brother. Holding the file in my hand, I opened the door and called out the last name for that day. An old lady with a lace shawl stood up from the bench. Her escort was a man, and when they walked into my small room, I saw who it was coming forward and was struck dumb.

"Oh—I never thought I would meet you here."

He said.

Clean white shirt.

Is it tonight or which night
That I see my fine man?

"I never thought I'd see you."

I said.

I pulled open the drawer in front of me and closed it again.

"We haven't met for so many years."

He said.

Corduroy trousers.

Now that I have seen my lord,
How can I fail to be at peace?

"About seven or eight years now."

He said.

I searched on the desk for the biro I had just been holding.

"It must be eight years."

He said.

Sandals.

Now that I have seen my lord,
How can I any more be sad?

The procedure for receiving an old – age pension is not very complicated, and it is even simpler when the applicants come in person to meet us. Our job is mainly to check their name, age and address, to examine their identity card and have a look at them. We just have to make sure they are still alive, and our job is done. I marked the checked items one by one and returned the various documents to the applicant.

''Are you Miss Fish?''

Old Mrs Chu asked.

''Is your surname really Yu—like the word for 'fish'?''

Old Mrs Chu asked.

Chu looked at his wristwatch.

''No. It's another Yu.''

I said.

''There was once an ancient emperor called Yu Shun. That's my name.''

I closed all the forms and the file, pulled out the drawer, closed it again and locked it.

''Are you going home now?''

He asked, supporting his aged mother, and adjusting her shawl.

''Yes, I go home for lunch after work.''

I said, walking ahead of them and opening the door of my small office.

''How about having lunch together?''

He asked.

A beautiful smile.

that clear-eyed man....

It was in the café that I caught the cold. It was really rather chilly inside the cafe. Or perhaps it was not then that I caught the cold, but in the following few weeks; Chu and I went to several cafés, and the air-conditioning invariably made us shiver. I had always had a good constitution, that was why I never took a coat with me. I was much too confident about my own resistance.

Chu often waited for me after work at the main entrance of my office building. We always went to have dinner together and drank coffee or red wine. Chu and I had endless things to talk about. We talked about our schooldays, that carefree, mischievous, proud time in our lives; we talked about innumerable fascinating episodes in our childhood; we talked about our present existence; it turned out that Chu had escorted his aged mother to our office because he and she were the only two people in their family.

Oh, soft and tender,
Glad I am that you have no friend.

"Had a lot of work recently?"

My mother said.

"Here are all your letters."

My mother said. So many letters, all from places doing business. They all said more or less the same thing—offered the most beautiful wedding gowns, the best photographers, the finest banquet services, and so on.

"Would you like to have roses or orchids for your bouquet?"

My mother said.

Ah—could I become a wisp of smoke?

"How about blue curtains for the new house?"

My mother said.

Ah—could I become a light breeze?

"Have you seen the ring they've sent over?"

My mother said.

Ah—could I become a drop of water?

"Your eldest cousin sent a silver cutlery service today."

Ah—could I turn into thin air?

I thought I ought not to meet Chu any more. I should definitely not go out with him to dinner again, or to the cinema. And yet I went. Why? The two of us were so very happy together. How would it end, if we went on like this? Wasn't I already engaged? Wasn't I getting married after the autumn?

South of the Yangtze the hills are so fine,
And now as blossoms fall I meet you once again.

I ought not to see Chu any more. So when he rang me up, I said I was exhausted and did not want to go out. When he rang again, I said I had a lot of extra work to do and did not have time. He could hardly be expected to believe my excuses, but I had no other way. To avoid meeting Chu, I even stayed inside the office toilet after work, until all the others had left. And then, after a long long wait, I came out alone. I thought that an hour would be enough, and he would have gone by then. But I should have known that Chu would not give up so easily, that he would persist until he had found me. So after waiting for over an hour, I came out and found Chu still standing there at the entrance of the building. I felt extremely awkward; I hung my head, like a guilty person.

"Why don't you want to see me?"

Chu said.

"What's all this about?"

Chu said.

When we were sitting again inside the café, my hand holding the cup began shaking uncontrollably. I could only tell him that we really had to part, because I was already engaged to somebody else and had to get married after the autumn. As a matter of fact, all sorts of wedding gifts had already started arriving at my house, I had even tried on my wedding gown. Everyone was working busily on my behalf, they had chosen a nice bridesmaid for me, a luxurious limousine, a fancy menu for the banquet. Everyone was so excited.

"You are only engaged."

Chu said.

"Just break off the engagement."

Chu said.

I thought, it was all to late. At this stage, what else could I do? My father had spent weeks busily arranging the wedding, he had accepted congratulations from countless people and, his face beaming with happiness, had begged his friends to come to the banquet. My mother was even busier, she looked as if she was about to buy the entire department store and bring it back with her. Our home was a scene of great merriment. And how, in the middle of all this, could I go and tell them I was not getting married after all? These people — my parents, their friends, my friend's parents, their relatives and friends — were they likely to let me get away with it so easily, with a casual "I'm not getting married"? I was trapped, I could never escape now.

"We can go away together."

Chu said.

"We can go and live somewhere else."

Chu said.

Could I just go away? Could I? Where would we go to? Yes, I could, Chu said; we could go to the furthest corners of the world. There would always be a place to go, as long as we could be together. But could I just go away?

At sunrise she bade her parents farewell,
At sunset she camped by the Yellow River;
She couldn't hear her parents call,
She only heard the River roar.

And my mother had high blood pressure, how would she take the shock? And how about old Mrs Chu? She would be left all alone when we were gone. Oh! Why did I ever consent to go out to lunch with Chu again? I should have gone home like a good girl for lunch, and then gone swimming with my brother.

"Why can't you give him up?"

Chu said.

"Because it's all too late."

I replied.

Oh, the River Han, so broad,
One cannot swim it!

"You are only engaged."

Chu said.

"So, it's all too late."

I said.

Oh, the River Jiang, so rough,
One cannot boat across it!

"Is it to repay a favour?"

I shook my head.

"Is it pressure from your parents?"

I shook my head.

"Is it for financial reasons?"

I shook my head.

"Is it because you are having his child?"

I shook my head.

"Even if you are, I won't mind."

My tears flowed.

We kept changing cafés, we kept walking down long streets. We circled round and round my house. Chu said he would rush in and tell my parents he was going to take me away. He said he would tell them he had to have me for his wife. I was so frightened: if Chu said he would do a thing, then he would do it. I knew what kind of a man he was. I could only beseech him.

"Please, I beg of you," I said, "don't do it."

"Please."

I said.

"Don't you like me?" Chu said, "Don't you like me any more?"

"Say that you don't like me," he said, "and I will go home straightaway."

But you did not provide for me—
Back to my home you sent me.

My tears flowed.

"Oh dear, Little Fish, how come you've got a cold again?"

My family doctor said to me. He was sitting on a rocking chair in our house. The rocking chair was his wedding gift for me. I had been married for more than three months now. He still called me Little Fish, although I was already somebody's wife now. I thought he was the only person in this world, apart from my family, who would never change his way of addressing me. Most of the others had already taken to calling me Mrs So and So. My doctor said to me: "How come you've got a cold again?" But as a matter of fact, I had never recovered from my cold in the first place. How I had disgraced my doctor!

On the day of my wedding, what kind of a bride was I ? A bride with an extremely heavy cold. I was dressed in my wedding gown, and in my hand I held a bunch of rose-coloured orchids and some tissues. Nobody can hide a cold, not even a bride. When my doctor posed with me at the church door for the photographer, in the presence of all those friends and relatives, I sneezed and sneezed. So my doctor said: "Dear me, I've never seen a bride with such a heavy cold." Then he squeezed my hand and winked at me, and said: "I think I'd better change professions and make wedding bouquets in future." The people who were standing there with me for the photograph did not quite understand what he meant, because they thought I had only just caught my cold; it was a cool autumn day and my wedding gown was so thin.

It was some festival or other and my family doctor had come to dinner with us. We had invited a few guests including my parents and my parents-in-law. All the men were talkers, the two women just smiled a lot. I had nothing much to say, so when they had a few drinks, I drank with them silently. I had become used to drinking silently.

Give me a drink to lighten the load.
As the cup is gilt, love is spilt.
Pain lasteth long.

When my doctor saw me drinking, he said cheerfully: "Come on, Little Fish, you ought to have a drink. You've got a cold, haven't you? Come on, let's drink a toast." So I picked up my glass again and drank a toast with him.

Drink deep of the rhino horn
But leave not love too long forlorn.

There was quite a festive atmosphere, but when all the guests had left, everything reverted to normal. Since my marriage, life had been very dull for me. Occasionally there were a lot of people in the house, but that only added smiles and voices. I often stayed in the bathroom by myself, sometimes staring blankly at my pale face in the painting-like mirror on the wall.

Why oil my hair...
Or pile it high,
If he come not forbye.

Sometimes I gazed at the second towel and toothbrush in the corner of the bathroom, and wondered how I had come to live with their owner.

My new environment gave me no joy. It was a totally unfamiliar place. The man living with me was very distant from me. We were so close, and yet so far apart. Why had my parents not wanted me? They did not want me, I was their abandoned child. It was they who had forced me to live in this place. Whose home was this?

Dove in jay's nest to bide...

I had no home. This place was not my home. If my heart could not dwell here, this could not be my home.

Dove in jay's nest at last...

And here I was, with someone I did not really want to live with. And why? When my husband held me in his arms, I felt so terrible, my heart was so sore. Why did I have to let those arms hold me? Then my tears flowed.

Then I looked about me and suddenly burst out weeping,
Because on that high hill there was no fair lady.

They flowed silently like a small stream, they flowed into my ears, and I heard my husband's voice: "Have I hurt you?"

At dawn she took leave of her parents,
At dusk she reached the head of Black River.
She heard not her parents call,
She only heard the Tartar horse whinny on
Swallow Mountain.

Who had hurt me? I had hurt myself. Why had I not left then? Why could I not have gone wandering out into the world with the man of my choice? And now it was all too late. I don't know how many times I had to tell myself every morning when I woke up—"Pluck up your courage, pull yourself up." It was too late to pull myself up now.

I dared write to Chu only some three months after my marriage.

I told him briefly that I was married, and he said in his reply: "For me, nothing has changed." But what could I do? Could we start all over again? For him, nothing had changed. My tears flowed again.

Ever since the onset of winter, I had been knitting a sweater for my husband. I knitted slowly, very slowly. I really was "at the window weaving".

Ask her who she longs for,
Ask her who she is thinking of.

I was stalling for time, I did not actually want to finish knitting the sweater, I was only knitting out of courtesy for my husband, not out of genuine feeling. But the others didn't understand, and my parents and my parents-in-law felt very comforted when they saw me employed in this fashion.

At Christmas time, my husband took me shopping specially to buy me a coat. But the softest coat could not make me warm. I really had made a mistake, taken a wrong path. But what could I do now? Only sit by the window and knit this sweater, this sweater I was not at all eager to finish. There was a light breeze outside, it seemed to be raining. What was Chu doing on this wintry evening? He said in his letter: "For me, nothing has changed." Ah!

The wind soughs sadly and the trees rustle.
I think of my lady and stand alone in sadness.

"Don't go and catch cold again."

My husband said. He closed the window for me, leaving a small crack, and wrapped a shawl around my shoulders. My husband was actually a warm, kind man. I thought perhaps I was being unfair to him. Perhaps I should try to be nicer to him in future, and we would be able to spend the rest of our lives quietly together, like other married couples.

"Don't go and catch cold again."

My husband said.

"You haven't got over your last cold."

My husband said.

No, I hadn't got over my cold. I think I will never ever get over it.

"Are you going to the hairdresser later?"

My husband said.

"Then I will go out with your brother, to look at some sports shoes."

My husband said.

The weather gradually grew warmer and I could go swimming again. Practically all winter I had spent indoors, and it was wonderful to be in the water again. My bones were reawakened. Hadn't my doctor told me: "Little Fish, you are a fish; swimming suits you." Yes, I was a fish. I belonged in the water. In a while, I might go to the hairdresser, but I was in no hurry to have my hair done. I might have it cut shorter for swimming, but I was not in any hurry. I only went to the hairdresser to have some time on my own.

My husband didn't like swimming. But he still used to come to the swimming-pool with me and my brother. He just dipped his pale body in the water, and when he came up his hair was not even wet. Now I could see him, sitting on a white iron chair beneath a beach-umbrella, drinking and reading the newspaper. The paper obscured his face. There were a lot of beach-umbrellas by the pool side, a lot of white iron chairs beneath the beach-umbrellas, a lot of people sitting on the chairs. There were a lot of people and my husband was lost in the crowd. I had had this feeling all along—I could not really distinguish my husband from the crowd, he was just a person I had met and lived with every day, a very unfamiliar person.

My brother swam in the pool with me, he swam very well; we were both like fish. How nice it was to be back in the water. I had not swum all winter, I had been feeling so tired, like a stranded fish, dry and dead.

And sooner or later you must share
In the making of grass.

But I wasn't dry, I wasn't dead. I was swimming in the water and felt an unspeakable sensation of happiness. I kept slowly swimming, I let the warm lazy water wrap itself around my body, I let the warm lazy sunshine fall on my back. I was so free, so easy, so unfettered. My brother was swimming alongside me all this time; and it seemed as if Chu was there too, floating and swimming by my side, as if we were swimming all the way out to sea, all the way out. We swam far, far, and then came back to lie on the beach in the sun. The happiest day in my life.

Last night, my husband went to a concert with me. He must have finally realised that I was too quiet and lonely, and decided to buy tickets for a concert. There are certain nights of the week when his friends always play mahjong together from late afternoon into the early hours. I just sit to one side and knit silently away at this sweater which I never want to finish. From time to time I serve them fresh tea.

Wasn't the friend who compared life to a pomegranate
Being a bit simple-minded?

During my knitting I can't help thinking—now I am over thirty; if I still have thirty years to live in this world, does that mean I am already halfway through my life? Will I be silently knitting and serving my husband's friends tea like this for the rest of my days? But I do want my husband and his friends to keep on coming and playing mahjong. If they don't, what can my husband and I talk to each other about? He's not Chu. On days other than mahjong days he and I just sit and watch endless drivel on the television.

The concert. My husband bought the tickets. I did not know which concert he had bought tickets for. When I asked what was on the programme, he just said: "Beethoven. You like Beethoven, don't you?" He doesn't actually understand music much, he doesn't get at all involved in it. I thought, if he could have chosen, he would certainly have preferred to stay at home and play mahjong with his friends. At yesterday's concert, the first item was Beethoven's Egmont Overture. This Dutch nobleman of the 16th century was executed for resisting the brutal tyranny of the Spanish ruler, the Duke of Alba. When his lover Klärchen learned of his death, she committed suicide. Egmont had a strange dream in prison; someone looking like Klärchen placed a victory wreath on his head.

Ah, the flowers—
Whose song is hidden in my heart?
In whose heart is my song hidden?

During the overture, when the victory theme recurred, I saw my husband yawn.

I don't know whether it was my husband's yawning or Mozart's Piano Concerto in B flat that made me feel so sad. Perhaps the two were connected. The Mozart first movement took me to some distant, desolate region. Then came the second movement, which had always been my favourite, such an earnest and touching piece of music, such a sad, melancholy journey into the depths of the soul. I don't know why but I suddenly found myself thinking about all that had happened to me during the past year. I felt myself to be a person with a soul—but then why had that soul taken leave of me and gone further and further away—that was probably why I felt so sad and melancholy. The third movement was a brisk, lively rondo, full of irony compared with the first two movements. Wasn't that in its turn a reflection of my present existence? I was living so quietly and peacefully, but I was so unhappy—that was an irony indeed.

During the interval, my husband seemed to feel relieved of a heavy load and went to have a drink in the foyer. I spotted Chu at once in the crowd, standing by the notice board. I knew that was where he would be standing if he had come. In the past, whenever we had arranged to go to a mime-show or a concert together, we would wait for each other at that spot. When Chu saw me, he smiled, and then the smile disappeared immediately from his face. It was because my husband was back at my side of course. Chu was much thinner than the last time I had seen him, which made me sad, but what could I do? I was helpless. He was wearing a dark blue anorak, a beautiful warm anorak. I had worn it before, so I knew.

The turtledove sings in the distance.
My dream sits in the birchtree.
"Miss Fish, you must have caught a cold."
Old Mrs Chu had said.
"Give your anorak to Miss Fish."
Old Mrs Chu had said.

So I knew it was a warm one. At Christmas my husband had given me an expensive soft Irish flannel coat. But I still felt cold in it. Even in a coat like that, which everybody thought so warm, I would not get over my cold. Chu had fallen ill; I knew he had, because he told me all about himself in the letters he had constantly been sending me. But I did not expect him to be so thin. I felt terrible and hung my head.

The second half of the concert was Beethoven's Fifth Symphony in C minor. Beethoven wrote other pieces in C minor, like his Coriolanus Overture, his "Pathetique" Sonata and his Third Piano Concerto. In his Fifth Symphony, the key of C minor somehow allowed him to give full rein to that passion and revolutionary fervour of his. I listened and it almost took my breath away. The music was so compelling, so strong and urgent, I seemed to see a Beethoven standing and crying before me—"Let me grasp Fate by the throat! I will not surrender to Fate!" I listened to Fate knocking at the door, from the ponderous beginning to the grand victorious finale. At that moment my soul soared with the music.

I don't know what my husband was feeling, sitting there in the concert hall. The clarinet solos, the andantes, the long crescendi on the strings, and then the announcement of the victory theme. What did it all mean to him? Wasn't I sitting in the concert hall with a log? To me, there in the concert hall, my husband was just a yawning log; no feelings, no response.

And it's no use eating spinach.

If Chu had been sitting beside me, how happy we would have been. Whenever he got excited, he would have held my hand tightly, we would have looked at each other and smiled; and then after the concert, on the ferry, we would still have been talking about Goethe and how he wrote his *Egmont,* and how Beethoven conquered his Fate.

It was already late when we walked out from the concert. I could still see Chu in the foyer, his eyes following me silently out of the main door of the hall. He did not smile at me again, but just gazed at me silently. I lost sight of him when I walked out of the glass door.

The turtledove sings in the distance.
The dream topples from the birchtree.

My husband and I walked over to the car in the carpark. Standing in the wide empty square, I raised my head and saw the crescent of the new moon in the sky. My husband saw me gazing up into the sky, and said: "Is it going to rain? We'd better hurry up." Ah—that's the kind of man my husband is.

"Here's a riddle for you."

Chu said.

"New moon. A famous line from a Tang poem."

Chu said.

"Any clues?"

I said.

"Is it an easy one?"

I said.

Gently consider, the
Beautiful city of Xianyang.

Beethoven's music is only to be found in heaven. The moon, the crescent of the new moon, "music for heaven". A few days earlier I had stood in front of the bathroom mirror and pulled out a white hair. My husband said: "I'll buy you a box of knotweed tomorrow. It will make your hair dark and shiny again." That's the kind of man my husband is. Didn't Chu once find a white hair on my head? But he said: "White is beautiful." A box of knotweed; that's my husband.

My husband is sitting at the pool side now. How obsessed he is with the business news!

The necessity of the evening papers,

the necessity of wearing flannel trousers,
the necessity of lottery tickets,
the necessity of rumours which thrive like weeds
from the other side of the stock exchange.

The newspaper submerges his head and face, I can only see his pale feet. Is this man sitting on the white iron chair my husband? I feel I don't actually know him; I can't identify his voice, I am not familiar with his footsteps, I've never watched his hands carefully, I have never taken in his features. I don't know what kind of watch he wears—is it a quartz automatic, does it give the date and the day of the week? I can't even say whether my husband wears glasses or not. And will I have to go on living with this man in this world for so many years to come?

How very very long a whole life is!

Am I not a well-educated woman living in the 1980s? After all these years of education, all these years of working in society, after watching so many different facets of life, what have I learned? How can I have become what I am?

Swimming is the only good thing. Swimming is such a strange experience, I feel so happy. When I swim past the side of the pool, water gushes out from the holes at the side, like Beethoven's music. Clarinets, eternal horns. Beethoven's Fifth Symphony—man can conquer Fate in the end. Everyday I tell myself when I open my eyes: have courage, and lift yourself up. But where is my true courage?

I am a fish. A fish. The current hits me. I know I am a fish. That piscine feeling has suddenly returned. I think I know how to be a lively fish. Didn't Chu once say: "You are a fish. Such a lively fish. 'A fish playing east of the lotus-leaves, west of the lotus-leaves, south and north of the lotus-leaves.' "

Yes, I am a fish; why do I have to be a stranded fish weeping by the river?

I come out of the swimming pool, the sunshine pours onto my shoulders and my hair. I feel an inexpressibly clear sensation in my whole body. Later my husband and my young brother will be going out to look at sports shoes. Then they will come back and stay here a bit longer. I can go my own way. My brother splashes my husband with water; he puts down his newspaper and sees that I have come out of the pool.

"Are you going?"

He says.

"Yes, I am going."

I say.

All of a sudden my voice is clear and strong, even I myself feel something strange about it. All winter, my throat has been hoarse and rough, my voice has been blurred and unclear. But now my voice is clear, my cold—can it have gone?

After only quarter of an hour, I am home, buoyant. No, this is not my home, it is my husband's home. This is my husband's home. Everything in the house, the tables, the chairs, the wardrobes, the floor, the ceiling, it all belongs to him. It is my husband's home. In my husband's home I have nothing. The only things I have are all the letters Chu sent me, beautiful letters full of true feeling. They are my only possessions. I brought them from my parents' home and have kept them in a travelling bag. Now all I have to take away with me is this bag. And the only reason I have for coming to this house again today is to collect the bag.

No matter on whose rafter the eternal nest is built
A peaceful acceptance, without clamour.

I hold the bag and stand in the street. Where to now? I don't know where to go. But there will be places. I am free now, a new person, full of life and joy. I walk down the long street, my step light and springing. I even think I may sing as I walk. Why is it so noisy over there? Oh, I remember now, it's a soccer ground. I can hear the cheering, they're watching a soccer match, they're in such high spirits. Why don't I watch as well? I've got plenty of time. Why don't I go as I am, with my bag, and watch the soccer match!

Have you seen the showers wet the leaves, the grass?
Be grass and leaf
Be shower

As you will

Oh, why not, why don't I just go as I am, with my great clumsy bag, and watch the soccer match!

The Drawer

Translated by Douglas Hui and John Minford

I have a drawer. I keep in it the little things I may need to use in the course of the day: coins, a bunch of keys, a watch, stamps, a half-empty packet of cigarettes. It's only a small drawer. Sometimes I pull it all the way out, tip it upside down and sort everything through. When I do this there's always a sound of something rolling away: a button, or a pencil stub. Rolling. From the desk down on to the floor, from the floor to some unknown place. If I can see it, I pick it up. If I can't, I just let it be.

When everything is tipped out of the drawer, some things do not roll; they just make a sort of clattering sound. It may be my lighter; or that tiny round mirror of mine. I can no longer remember how that little mirror got into my house, how it has managed to monopolize that corner of the drawer for so long. I only know that it has become part of my life. Every day without fail, when I open the drawer I see it. And once I see it, a voice seems to rise from some strange place: Hallelujah, we are alive.

I go to work every day. Even on Sundays, I have somewhere to go. That's why I have to open my drawer every day. I have to open it for my purse, my cigarettes, my keys, and my ID card. Each time I open the drawer, I see my mirror lying face-up in the corner, like an unruffled little pool of water. And in the mirror, I see myself.

No one else has ever opened my drawer. Other people have their own drawers. My drawer is entirely mine. In that little drawer of mine lives my mirror; and in my mirror, me. It's become a habit with me now, after all this time, not to rush straight to my keys or purse first thing when I open the drawer. And I'm in no hurry to put my lighter and cigarettes into my pocket. Instead, I glance quickly at the mirror lying in the corner of the drawer, to see if I am there or not. The mirror has never failed me; I always know I'm not lost, I have been living in my drawer all along, safe and sound.

In point of fact, after all this time, now, whenever I open the drawer, what I see is no longer a mirror, but me. Oh, that must be my nose... And those are my ears on either side of it... I feel comforted: I know that both my nose and my ears have been living peaceful, comfortable lives in my drawer all along. And I push the drawer lightly in, so as not to disturb their peace and quiet.

For many years I have not known where I am, and have been much afflicted by melancholy as a consequence. I have not known where I am in this infinite universe. But gradually I have come to know. Very gradually. I have finally arrived at the truth of the matter through all my daily openings of the drawer. The fact is, I have been living all along in my drawer. The knowledge that I actually have a place of domicile in this universe has brought me an incomparable sense of happiness. No more need for me to lament the futility of life, to see myself as a drifting soul, a passing phantasm.

By the side of my mirror in the drawer lies my ID card. Every day, before I leave home, I open the drawer, take out the ID card and put it in my pocket. Then I take out one or two other bits and pieces—my purse, my ball-point pen, and so on and so forth. When I return from the outside world, I open the drawer again, put back the ID card by the mirror, and then place the odds and ends of the things that I use in the day back in the drawer, one by one.

The other day I went shopping for a pair of shoes. I chose the type of shoe I wanted, and the salesman asked me if I'd brought my pattern with me. That suddenly made me think of an ancient fable. I said to him, do you take me for an idiot? What do you think today is, April Fool's day? Why should I need to bring my pattern with me to buy shoes? I've brought my feet. Look! But the salesman insisted on my producing my pattern. They only accepted patterns, not feet. What good were feet? That was what they said. You could only prove something about your feet by producing your pattern. Your pattern had a photo of your feet on it, it had your toe prints, the date of birth of your feet, their race and nationality, their colour, their names and aliases in Chinese and English, their shape and measurements. And their Civil Registration Number. What good were your actual feet? Only your pattern could prove that your feet were yours.

This encounter taught me that my pattern was my feet. In a similar manner, I have learnt that my ID is me. So I put my ID away in my drawer every day with extraordinary care. My drawer is my only domicile in this infinite universe, and I must protect it as best I possibly can. I worry about my house catching fire, about hurricanes and storms, about earthquakes. These calamities would mean ruin for my drawer. If my drawer were gone, where would I be able to be? If the drawer were gone, my ID would be gone too; if my ID were gone, I would be gone too. Likewise, if the drawer were gone, so would my mirror; if my mirror were gone, so would I. No wonder I have taken out such an expensive insurance policy for my drawer.

That's it. For so many years, I haven't known who I am, where I am, where I come from or where I'm going to. I have thought hard about all these questions, but to no avail. Now I've got the answers. The questions that have perplexed me for so many years have vanished like wisps of smoke. I don't have to ask any more who I am, where I am, where I come from, where I am going to, how I should go on living. I am not troubled by these questions any more.

Who am I? I have only to open my drawer and my ID tells me who I am, in great detail. Where am I? Again, I only have to open my drawer and look into my mirror. Haven't I been living comfortably in my mirror all along? Haven't I been keeping my mirror carefully in the drawer all along? Where am I? In my drawer, of course. It hardly needs saying. As for where I come from, from the Immigration Department, of course. And where am I going to? To the Registry of Births and Deaths, of course.

Yesterday, I ran into some friends of mine on the street. They'd arranged to have coffee together at a café, and asked me whether I would like to join them. Like to? I said. How could I know? I'd have to go home and consult my drawer. And then they asked me whether I would go swimming with them on Sunday. I said I didn't know that either. I'd have to go and consult my drawer.

That's it. If you ask me whether I like lying in the sun on the grass, I have to go and consult my drawer. If you ask me whether the apple I'm eating is sweet, I have to go and ask my drawer. If you ask me whether I am happy or not, I have to go and ask my drawer.

May 1981

Toys

Translated by Douglas Hui and John Minford

They had many toys: tin soldiers, teddy bears, musical boxes, and miniature motor boats. In the park, they fetched out their toys and placed them on the grass. They put the teddy bears and musical boxes on the park bench and the miniature motor boats in the pond.

—Bring your toys.

—Let's play together.

They said. So I brought the dangling bell you gave me, the gadget with pieces of ice hanging from tiny strings. As I walked, the ice pieces knocked against each other and gave out a tinkling sound. I also brought the ice-fish I had carved myself. I had told them my toys were something new. I carved them carefully by hand and each one was different from the last. But they didn't see; they didn't believe.

On the way to the park, little by little the ice-fish melted away; the water dripped on the ground from between my fingers. At first, the tail faded away; then the whole body dwindled, becoming thinner and thinner until finally it was no more than a shapeless stick of ice, and then it vanished entirely. The dangling bell shared the same fate, leaving bits of bare string tied to a narrow piece of wood. What kind of a toy was that? They said.

They exchanged all sorts of toys in the park. They preferred more substantial objects. I could only tuck the strings that hung from my hand into my pocket and go running alone on the grass. The breeze dried my still dripping hands.

Afterwards, I grew up. I saw many kinds of exhibitions in

exhibition rooms. I saw brass and iron, fibreglass and granite, tree trunks and concrete; all substantial, and fashioned into different shapes. Standing there, each object was real as anything, its features visible. You could reach out your hands and touch them. Colour, texture, form, abstract and concrete, everything there neat and clear, and a label below each of the pieces. It made me think of you.

How can you exhibit your ice sculptures? If you put one of your huge jugs, or one of those strange masks of yours, on show in an exhibition hall, people will see nothing. They will say, what sort of sculpture is this? They will turn away and look for something more substantial. But you don't work for substance, or for some large exhibition; you don't work for a crowd of spectators, or to provide material for the critics. That's why you said you were happy, and free from care.

He lived just a floor below her at that time. On her way down, if the door was ajar, she would see him standing in a corner by the window, a knife and chisel in his hands, carving.

He moved great lumps of ice from the market. He put the ice on a four-wheeled cart and pushed it rumbling along the road. The ice was covered with jute sacks, and as they soaked up the water, they changed colour from straw to walnut. She always stood at the main entrance of the building, watching him lug up the ice and move it indoors. Then she followed him into the house.

It was usually cool inside his room. Sometimes, upon entering the room, all she could see was a long four-legged table and a wooden bench. The room was dimly lit. But there were times when she entered the room to find it filled with bright crystalline ice-sculptures. Here, a huge jug. There, a whole wall of masks. Each piece of ice transparent as glass. They really shone, she said. So he made her a dangling ice-bell, several small bits of ice suspended from a cluster of strings. When the strings swayed, the bits of ice knocked against each other and made a tinkling sound.

Occasionally, he would give her a small piece of ice of her own and a nail, or a key, and let her try her hand at a tiny ice fish or a leaf shaped like a hand. When she touched the ice, she felt a cold beauty in it. By the next day the ice would always have melted away. The tiny fish and the leaf that she had made would have slowly become water. Even the large jugs and the weird masks melted by degrees. As they melted, their shapes changed imperceptibly. The mouths of the jugs twisted to one side. The masks grew long beards on their chins. To her, these were all new delights.

When all the ice had melted away, the room became drab and dark once more. She would ask: What will it be tomorrow? He would tell her that it would be a flying fish, or a sea-horse, or an ice xylophone. She would ask: Will I be able to make a big jug like yours when I grow up? She described a circle in the air with her hands. Then he laughed and said: Oh, definitely, definitely, a jug bigger than that, even more beautiful.

You sell fish. You are a fishmonger, and you carve ice. I have no idea whether you started off as a fishmonger and did your ice-carving later, or whether you began as an ice-sculptor and sold fish afterwards. It must be an interesting story. But you say it makes no difference which came first.

I like watching you carve, and I like watching you sell fish. In the morning market, the ground is all water, especially in front of the fish stall. People make their way past, rubbing shoulders against each other. Sometimes, a shopping basket catches a thread of wool in my coat and almost pulls me away. Sometimes, a spray of watercress scratches my face, sharp as a knife. But I always stand in front of the wooden bucket, watching you sell your fish. My feet must get all splashed and dirty, you say.

I enjoy watching the fish swim in the bucket. A hose sprays water on to the bodies of the fish. The drops are the colour of ice. But when they fall into the water, they don't shine like crystal any more. If there's a white fish-maw floating on the top of the bucket, I know a fish has turned over. Sometimes, a white shrimp can be seen zigzagging in the bucket, its body almost transparent, as if it too is carved from ice. And then, often, quite suddenly, it disappears in the water, as if it too, like an ice shrimp, is melting away.

Lying on the table are fish that will swim no more. Around them, broken pieces of ice, which make the whole table glitter. The customers pick up a fish, turn up its gills, press its belly, and then inspect its eyes; some of them may even hold it up to their noses and smell it, like an orchid. You weigh each fish they choose, scrape the scales off with your toothed scaler, and cut out the inedible parts with a knife. Then you wrap it up in newspaper and tie it with a reed.

With the fish scales dancing around you, you really look as if you are carving. The small chips of ice go flying around you in the same profusion. They are just as brilliant, as aqueous, as chilly. That is why I like watching you sell fish. You are not actually selling fish, are you? You are still carving. Only instead of ice, you've got a live fish in your hand. No, no, I'm selling fish, you say.

Once a man taking a census asked me: What does the man living below you do? Other people say, he sells fish. I answered:

— He carves.

— He carves ice.

The man wrote down "fishmonger" on his paper—you happened to come home just at that moment. They asked you, and you said you sold fish. We argued about it afterwards, when you were carving me a mask. But you handed me a piece of ice and tapped me on the head. You said: Don't you want to let me sell fish? My eyes reddened, and I said: No, no, I like you selling fish. And I added: When I grow up, I want to sell fish too, just like you.

March 1976

Asuo

Translated by Maria Chi
and John Minford

Her arms are aching. Little Wuwu is really growing so much heavier all the time, He didn't seem so heavy a few days ago. But today all of a sudden he is somehow heavier. Tomorrow, and the day after, little Wuwu will keep on growing heavier. And then Asuo will not be able to hold him in her arms any more.

Little Wuwu is a very good child and seldom cries. When Asuo holds him in her arms and the sun shines directly into his eyes,he lets his head fall. Sometimes he rests his head on Asuo's shoulder and sleeps. Perhaps it is because he is so good that the uncles asked Asuo to hold him and stand over here on this side of the grassland. When Asuo first stood with him here, he was tiny, just like a little Hami melon. But now he is more like a little lamb.

Asuo's home is on the other side of the mountain, in the pine forests. There is a great stretch of green, green grassland there too. The uncles brought Asuo here and asked her to hold Little Wuwu in her arms and stand at the entrance to the tent. She doesn't need to do anything or go anywhere else. Asuo's family live in a yurt too. The uncles who speak a strange language call the tent a *meng-gu bao*.

The uncles who speak the strange language are different from the uncles who speak Asuo's language. Their eyes and noses are not the same. Asuo's father says that she cannot understand their speech because they are Han Chinese. Asuo and her family are Kazakhs. Kazakhs live in yurts.

The uncles first told Asuo to stand at the entrance of this tent a long time ago. This tent is much more beautiful than Asuo's home. There are coloured flower-patterns on the rugs and hangings. The colours are so clear, it is so bright inside the tent: the mirrors and boxes can be seen quite plainly. The rugs in Asuo's home have fewer flowers. They are old and the patterns are worn and faded.

The carpets and the embroidered bedspreads inside this tent look very beautiful to Asuo, so bright and clean. Probably that's because there is nobody living there, and nobody sleeping there at night. Nobody eating roast lamb and drinking sheep's milk. In Asuo's home, there's the smell of sheep's milk, oil stains and smoke stains everywhere.

Asuo cannot understand why the uncles have to put up this beautiful tent with nobody living in it, why they have asked her to stand by the entrance all day with Little Wuwu in her arms. Standing at the entrance of the tent, Asuo has to put on her prettiest clothes and shoes, her prettiest hat. Little Wuwu has to wear his prettiest clothes and shoes, and his prettiest hat. But Asuo likes to wear pretty clothes, especially her hat with the feathers and the bright ruby earrings. Sometimes Asuo feels as pretty as the rugs in the tent, and she is very happy. But her arms ache from holding Little Wuwu all day long.

There is great excitement on the slope at the other side; some of the uncles are racing horses. They are all riding horses, galloping. And some of the younger uncles are being chased and whipped by some of the younger aunties, who are also on horseback. When those young uncles are whipped, they never cry out, they laugh even though they feel pain. Asuo would like to watch the racing and the whipping, but she cannot go there to watch because the uncles have told her to stand at the entrance to the tent with Little Wuwu in her arms, and not to go anywhere else.

On the grassland in front of the tent, a little distance from it, some uncles are boiling water in a pot on a stove. There are large basins and pans spread all around on the grass. Asuo can see smoke rising from the stove. Further away on the grass, there is a new stove with four legs, like a low table. Charcoal is glowing on it red and grey, for roasting lambs. Asuo likes to watch the lambs roasting. They put the lamb on a spit, and turn it round and round over the fire until the smell of the roasted meat is wafted everywhere. Asuo likes to eat lamb and drink sheep's milk. But she can't go to watch the lamb roasting because the uncles have told her to stand by the entrance to the tent with Little Wuwu in her arms, and not to go anywhere else.

Asuo stands by the tent, and all the time she sees the uncles and aunties who speak the strange language, looking at her curiously and saying something she does not understand. Sometimes, they examine her clothes closely, her shoes, her hat, her eyes, nose and mouth; sometimes they examine Little Wuwu's shoes, his hat, his eyes, nose and mouth. And some of the aunties like to touch the feathers on Asuo's hat. All these uncles and aunties like to take photos of Asuo, so Asuo smiles and asks Little Wuwu not to let his head fall. They like to go inside the tent. First they stand in the entrance and poke their heads in to look around, pointing at the rugs, the hangings, the mirrors and the boxes. They are excited and their voices are raised; it's just like when a sheep is grabbed in the horseraces. Then they like to go inside and they all sit on the ground. They ask Asuo to sit with them and one of the uncles goes to the door and takes a photo of them all together. When they take the photo, Asuo smiles and tells Little Wuwu not to sleep with his head on her shoulder.

This is the only time Asuo can sit on the ground and put Little Wuwu down next to her. It's the only time her arms stop aching. One of the uncles may give Asuo an egg; she takes it gently and holds it in her hand. Asuo still feels her arms aching a little when she holds the egg. She does not know why.

The uncles and aunties go as quickly as they came. After they have gone, Asuo takes Little Wuwu in her arms once more and stands at the entrance. Little Wuwu is growing up and Asuo will not be able to carry him for much longer. But then the uncles will ask her to hold Little Kashi instead, because he is smaller than Little Wuwu. And when Little Kashi grows up, they will ask her to hold Jimusal, because he is younger than Little Kashi, and then there is Asisi who is even younger than Jimusal.

Of course, Asuo will grow up too. But she feels she is growing very slowly. When will she really be grown up? Then she won't have to stand at the entrance of the tent with a baby boy in her arms any more; she'll be able to ride the horses like her older sisters and the young women. Asuo likes the racing.

On the far slope, some of the uncles are grappling for a sheep. Asuo can tell, just by listening to the sound of the horses' hooves. There are a lot of them galloping across the grassland after a sheep. When two of them grapple for the same sheep, each one takes hold of a leg and pulls with all his might. The aim is to get hold of the greatest number of sheep. Asuo would like to watch them grappling for the sheep, but she has to stand at the entrance of the tent with Little Wuwu in her arms, and is not allowed to go anywhere else. The sun is shining on Little Wuwu's bonnet; he is sleeping on Asuo's shoulder. Asuo feels her arms aching. Little Wuwu is really growing so much heavier all the time.

Maria

Translated by Douglas Hui and John Minford

I

"This is Radio Stanleyville. Today is the twenty-fourth of November, 1964."

Maria's eyes were wide open. Beside her, a nun was praying, her face obscured from sight. It was very dark in the room. From beyond the wall came the sound of a transistor radio—the radio of the rebels. The rebels were outside; the rifles were outside.

"This is Radio Stanleyville. Here once again are the main points of the news. The Kenyan government has warned the Belgian authorities and the United States not to interfere in any way in the internal affairs of the Congo. If the two countries attempt to attack Stanleyville, they may be sure that retaliatory measures will be taken. The Congo belongs to the Congolese."

The Congo is ours.

Looking out from the darkness, from here to there, from this wall to that wall, nothing but people standing. To the right a small window, and through it a tiny patch of sky. People crowding up against it, struggling to catch a glimpse of the blue beyond. Beyond, beyond the window, the whole world, and due south, the Congo River. But at this moment, now, beyond the window, a formation of rifles.

"A radio broadcast from Leopoldville has reported a Belgian government statement issued on Friday night: Belgian marines are ready for action any time to rescue the white hostages imprisoned by the rebels in Stanleyville. According to a statement by the Belgian Ministry of Foreign Affairs, a battalion of marines has already arrived at Ascension Island, 1266 nautical miles off the west coast of Africa, and is on standby alert there. The statement also said that, with the support of the U.S. Air Force, this first battalion of Belgian marines would mount a rescue operation on purely humanitarian grounds. Premier Tshombe said this morning that..."

All of sudden the door opened. A Congolese rebel, tall, dark and fierce, towered above them, roaring like a gorilla:

"Out!"

Out they all went, all of them in that small room. Maria made an exact tally: sixteen nuns, twenty-three priests, three persons of unknown occupation, altogether forty-three, including herself. She had been counting them silently just now in the dark, like sheep. One, two, three, four.... They all looked so desperate, as though this was Imperial Rome, and they were about to be thrown to the lions.

We are lions; Africa is our home.

Yes, they were face to face with lions. The rebels called themselves lions, they called themselves *shaba;* and they looked like wild beasts. When Maria was first sent to the Congo in 1954, she had been in charge of a Catholic hospital at Pandaba, three hundred miles northwest of Stanleyville. Next to the hospital, she also set up a girls' school. All the girls in the neighbourhood went to her school. They were all very dark: one had big eyes, one had very white teeth, one had a miserable look—they were all imprinted on Maria's memory. Maria also remembered that it was time for the beasts to roar.

"Divide up!"

The gorillas were roaring. One of them pointed towards a patch of muddy ground, asked those with any medical knowledge to stand there, and ordered the rest to face the wall. They all knew what was coming. The nuns huddled together and cried out with staring eyes:

"Kill us all together! We won't be separated!"

But lions know how to sort out the sheep from the goats. Lions are wise, like leopards. Yes, that's it, leopards. On the fifteenth of last September, a band of rebels dressed in leopard-skins broke into Maria's school. "You are spies working for the Americans," they said. They took a lot of things away. They took the radio away. The students all fled; not a single patient dared come to the hospital again after that. But the leopards kept coming. Ever since war latched onto this land, armies had come, and gone, and come again; fighting had flared up, died down, and flared up again. A United Nations force had come once and halted the rampant gunfire for a time, but no country would give them support and so the bankrupt army withdrew. And then the leopards came. They had been coming from September of last year to September of this year; they kept coming, snatching sheep, stealing chickens and making off with rice. "We'll pay," they said, but they never did. It was like a song. Once sung, it was ended. No one can be held responsible for a song that has ended.

"Divide up!"

Said the leopard. No one could fail to hear it. The rebels came over at last, using their rifle-butts to divide the crowd. Maria was pushed onto the muddy ground, like a desolate little blade of grass growing on the deck of a ship. The lions faced the wall and took aim. And then the rifles fired.

Time passed, time was, and then the rifles fired. Maria was a desolate blade of grass. The lions began to push their way into an army truck; the back of the truck was full of desolate blades of grass. Maria sat by the window. Before long the truck started and she watched the trees go by the window one by one, counting them like sheep: one, two, three, four. A monotonous sound came from outside: the rumbling of the truck wheels, other sounds beyond the wheels.

"Radio Stanleyville. On his ranch President Johnson has held his first press conference since winning the presidental election. He says he has no intention of meeting either the new Soviet leaders or President De Gaulle. He does not think that the Atlantic Alliance is compatible with a narrow sense of nationalism and self-interest. As regards the Congo, the President said, there is no political animosity on the part of America. The United States only hopes to see Africa restored to peace, stability and order, after four years of confusion and political struggle.''

Africa: whose is Africa?

The wheels rumbled; beyond the wheels, other sounds, distinct sounds, coming from overhead. It must be a plane. The lions had no planes; Johnson had planes, so did Tshombe. Day in, day out, Johnson and Tshombe sent their reconnaissance planes on patrol over Stanleyville, each one in a convoy with two jet fighters. Now they must be taking aerial photographs of the woods and main roads. They were making quite a din. But Maria did not see them. She was still counting the trees outside.

The trees soon ended. Maria started counting houses. Familiar houses; Stanleyville houses. Rue Baro. Rue Potin. On, on—that must be the Place Lumumba ahead, with the statue of Lumumba, the rebels' Christ, in the middle. There was such a huge gulf between Lumumba and Maria's idea of Christ. But it could be reduced to a single difference: Lumumba liked war, Christ did not.

The truck stopped short, and Maria's heart sank; there she was, face to face with the statue of Lumumba. ''Divide up!'' The scene flashed before her eyes again. But why here this time? Why bring them to the Place Lumumba? Before she had time to think it out, the truck had already stopped, and the sound of the planes grated on their ears. The outside world seemed suddenly to have been transformed into a Niagara Falls, reverberating with a deadening roar. Someone got off the truck. Time passed, time was. The truck door was suddenly forced open, and three nuns jumped down. Where had it come from, that huge throng of people outside? Outside, there was still a sky, a sky that bloomed with one flower after another, like red balloons, like waves churned out from a red mill. A thousand voices were seething, and then the thousand voices merged into one cry, and Maria heard it:

''The marines have come!''

The marines have come. They must be coming to rescue us. Of course. We are sheep; the marines have come to rescue the sheep, so that the lions can't eat them any more. Thousands of sheep fleeing in one direction. Escaping. They didn't love Stanleyville any more. They didn't love the waters and woods here any more. Maria chose the Congo in 1954, she loved the Congo. Many other nuns and priests had come, they too said they had come to give their love to the Congo, to its flowering seasons, to its tears. But now, they didn't love the Congo any more.

Who really loves the Congo?

Have the marines come? They must be Belgian. Belgium is in Europe, so is France. How close to each other the two countries are. France was Maria's home. But a nun has no home. When Maria was a child, her piano teacher had told her that a musician had no weekends. It was more or less the same. It's November: are the seagulls still in Marseilles? It must be very quiet in the Rue des Roses in Paris by now. But in the Latin Quarter, the long-haired girls play their guitars all the year round.

The truck bounced as the people in the rear jostled with one another to jump off; and the lions were roaring. Then Maria heard the rifle-fire, bursts of rifle-fire, and then corpses were dumped in the main street like dogs. But voices could still be heard:

"It's the Belgian marines. They have come to rescue us. To the airport quick!"

The words were uttered to the tramping of feet. The sound overhead grew particularly fierce. She could not distinguish all the sounds, but this was not music. She could distinguish music, but not noise. The noise of the rushing crowd filled the street like a downpour of rain. There was no let-up from the guns; the heavy machine-guns thundered, the light guns sputtered, the pistols barked. Maria could see people, all flying towards the airport as if they had wings.

They have all gone. No one loves the Congo. And me? A young mother in her pyjamas, a blue-eyed child with bare feet. To them, the Congo means nothing. And me? What about me? Maria had nowhere to go, she had only a place to come to, and she had already arrived. The Congo, France; grapes, bananas.

What made you become a nun?

There were so many flowers in the sky. They were blooming right there above the airport. The truck started up again some time or other, full of lions. "Have the Belgian marines come?" Maria asked a rebel.

The truck sped past the houses, away from the Congo River, towards the northeast. Lumumba's statue was left behind. The paintings of Goya. The red of Matisse.

"Have the Belgian marines come?" Maria asked.

Lions were all around her. They all had three eyes, two in their head, one in their gun. A rebel sitting opposite her spat a mouthful of saliva out of the window at a badly decomposed corpse on the roadside and said contemptuously:

"The marines have come. Why didn't you run for it?"

"She's got no guts. She's afraid of death," another rebel put in, without even turning his head.

II

He was very young. Altogether they had caught three; he was the youngest, and the only one still alive.

"Can someone give me water, please." He spoke in French with a southern accent. Maria knew straightaway that he was French; from his curly hair, and his short thick-set physique. The lions had kept him manacled all morning. Several times he asked "Can someone give me water, please", but no one paid any attention; some could not understand what he was saying, some were too apathetic. The lions paid no attention to the plane overhead either. The clock went on relentlessly ticking.

They had caught three today. Early in the morning, in a confused skirmish, seventeen of the lions died. So they raged with all the rage they had ever known. They cut the throats of the hostages, and sucked their blood; then they ripped open their bellies, took out the guts and laid them out in the sun. But the lions bled too. Maria was helping a lion to bandage a bullet hole on his forehead. What a lot of blood poured from it. Lions bleed too of course. They care about their lives too. This lion was panting now, but still he grasped his rifle in one hand, pressing the other against the wound on his head. Maria ripped the hem off her dress and bandaged him up with it. It made him look just like an Arab.

The Congolese and the Arabs have the same destiny. Arabia does not belong to the Arabs; the Congo does not belong to the Congolese. The Congo has over eighty tribes, and more than one hundred and sixty dialects. It is the largest country in Africa. But there is widespread enmity between the different tribes. They like shedding blood. They are stubborn and incorrigibly superstitious. They are cruel and ruthless. It is just like Arabia, just like the Middle East during the Second World War. Each Congolese is a sun, scorching this vast tract of land.

How many suns are there altogether, scorching this vast tract of land?

"Damn the plane!" The wounded lion bellowed impatiently. "Damn the plane! Damn the white men!" He ran over to the hostages, gave them a good working-over with the butt of his rifle, then went back and sat under a tree, cursing to himself repeatedly, until it started to sound like a chant. But he quietened before long. In the end, he put his rifle on the ground and took out a lamp. He lit the lamp and began burning a strange-smelling herb over it. It was marijuana from India. He sat there inhaling it. The plane buzzing above the treetops like a mosquito annoyed him.

The hostage made no more noise. Maria had no water. To the left of them was a small river, where all the lions drank. They each had a water bottle. Maria had none. The hostage wanted water. What an idea of his, to want water. The lions wanted his blood. It was strange that the lions hadn't killed him. But one could never be sure; they might do it tonight. They were sick of the sight of his face. Tonight, they might cut him into slices, as if they were slaughtering a sheep, and cheer afterwards like their hunting ancestors. He was a sheep. He was also a turkey. The lions had caught three turkeys today. Maria had no idea what date today was. But surely it could not be the twenty-fourth of November. The day of the massacre had passed. A water-bag in the desert; one tilt and it would all be gone. Today might be Christmas Eve. But so what if it was? Would the war end because of that? The war might pause, only to surge again like a flood afterwards. And the plane overhead had not ceased for a moment, nor had the gunfire.

"Water," said the hostage.

A lion came over and splashed a bottle of water onto his face. He opened his mouth wide, but the water was already gone. All around him the lions let out a roar of laughter. How their laughter echoed. But soon it took on an unlaughterlike quality. For a louder echo was heard, like a volcano erupting; everyone heard it. It was very near, and very loud. It was something beyond a bomb, or an earthquake. Later the sound modulated into a series of crackling explosions. Flames rose in the distance, smoke, wind, cries. The rebels changed their position. A crowd rushed over.

"Why don't you just drop down out of the sky, you damned plane!" The smoking lion blew out the lamp and took his rifle. But he couldn't stand up, and went on leaning against the tree.

People rushed over, lots of people. They materialized all of a sudden. Maria didn't know there were so many people in the vicinity. They must have all been hiding behind the trees, one behind each tree. Now in a split second the whole wood was moving. The lions were out hunting again. The smoke outside was very thick, the noise outside was deafening. The smell of burning came wafting over.

"I'll go and fetch you some water," Maria said to the hostage, looking everywhere for a container. But there was only grass all around; and apart from grass, trees.

"What is this place?" he asked.

"The Equator. The Congo. Wamba."

"Is it near Stanleyville?"

"Stanleyville's to the southwest, two hundred and fifty miles away."

Maria couldn't find a thing. Not a can, not a length of pipe, not even a piece of scrap metal. There was a din in the distance. Everyone was over there. They were all there! Maria turned abruptly and said to the hostage.

"Now's your chance. Can you run?"

But the hostage shook his head, his eyes gazing in front of him. Maria followed his line of vision. There were countless gun barrels pointing at them. They would never be able to escape. Anyway, lions are not lions for nothing. The trees concealed them. The shade covered their faces.

"Besides, I don't want to escape," he said.

"You are not a priest. You are a soldier."

"I am not an ordinary soldier; I am a mercenary. They give me a rifle, give me money; I give them my life. I'm a professional fighter. I can leave today, but tomorrow I'll be back again. We are always meeting each other in the battlefield. It's just like travelling. We are shadows of each other, we follow each other. Death is not so very different from life. Today it's me, tomorrow it's you. It depends on your luck."

What made you become a mercenary?

"Where are you from?"

"Paulis first, then Kindu, Bukavu, then Stanleyville."

"What's it like in Leopoldville?"

"The marines took the hostages there. They sat in the airport wailing. Some of them were barefoot, some were in their pyjamas. There were doctors and nurses from the Red Cross to give them medical treatment. After that the United States put them on the planes they had used to transport the marines, and flew them to Brussels. They made several journeys. The King and Queen of Belgium were at the airport to greet them."

"It's a desert here. All the news is dead news."

"The marines left Stanleyville on the twenty-ninth of November. But the war did not end. They have rescued over a thousand Whites, but in Africa plenty of others have died. Besides, there is trouble all over the world, not just in Africa.

Students have destroyed the U.S. Embassy in Moscow. The same thing has happened to the British, American, and Belgian embassies in Czechoslovakia and Romania. Even in Egypt, a mob has destroyed American buildings in Cairo and set fire to the Kennedy Memorial Library. It makes me think of Caesar. He set fire to Cleopatra's library."

"What about the United Nations?"

"It's too weak. They just hold meetings, meetings. The U.S. Ambassador Stevenson said in the General Assembly that America's action was a humanitarian one; but Kenya and some other African countries called it aggression. The politicans have gone to great lengths to move the war from the battlefield to the conference table, but conferences have never solved any problems. The Geneva Conference tried to settle the Indochina problem in 1954, and it's still there today. The crisis in South-east Asia is still continuing. It's not a war between men; it's a war between political ideologies. It's the politicians and the militarists who wage war, the soliders and civilians just die in it. Look, the rebels are coming back again. Go and ask them why they are fighting. They don't even know themselves."

The rebels were coming back. There were metallic sounds in the wood, and footsteps. They all wanted to give their own description of the scene at once.

"It was an American."

"I heard him cry 'Help, help!' It was definitely English."

"The blaze set his hair alight. Actually, we could have dragged him out."

"I could have finished him with one shot. But he was a white man, an American. I wanted to see how he burnt alive."

"It was a D-C 4 transport, not a C-130 fighter."

"Not one of Tshombe's T-6 fighters either."

"What was a transport doing here?"

"That was just his bad luck. This is war."

Yes, this is war. The young hostage told Maria that war would never end, that peace was an unreachable fruit. She suddenly thought of the water again. She went over and asked for water from a wounded rebel. He thought for a minute and then unfastened his water-bottle and gave it to her. She handled it with great care, but another lion ran over and snatched it away, pouring the water to wash the mud from his feet. Maria stood motionless for a while, then walked back to the hostage. The lions encircled them.

She started gnawing at the rope that tied him. The rebels laughed heartily as if they were watching a performing monkey. A rebel ripped open her clothes. But she kept gnawing away, biting through one strand of rope at a time. The rope gave a little. Then she tore at it with all her might, and it broke in two. She helped the hostage to stand up. He stood with his back bent at first, but managed to straighten it before long. She brushed the dust from his body for him and began to lead him forward. The lions all stared at her. By and by they were staring at her with all three eyes. She walked in front. He did not say a word, but tottered lamely behind her. The small river flowed across their path not far ahead. After a few steps, Maria turned round and saw his face suddenly brimming with sunshine. He was smiling gaily, and began to speak in a very tender voice.

''You know? I can always remember Corsica. Corsica is in the very south, even farther south than Marseilles. Napoleon lived there. Corsica is my home. I can remember how it looks in mid-summer. There are flowers and trees everywhere. You have to make your way through the undergrowth if you come down from the hills. There are different kinds of trees: tall pines, straight oaks, chestnuts, beeches. Corsica is a small island jutting out of the sea. It's just like Aphrodite rising from the waves. Even the wind, and the sunshine. High on the mountains, you can find red bayberries, rosemary, yew and juniper. By the sea, artemisia grows under your feet. And all around you asphodel, fennel, pomegranate. And marsh grass and white flowering shrubs. Corsica is a huge garden. Apart from the flowers, there is the sea, and the mountains which rise straight from the sea. There are no beaches, but there are cactuses transplanted from Africa. And the sunshine is always blinding. Between the rocks grow the rock roses. The grass has a slightly pink tint. In those days, I used to wish I had ten francs. I used go fishing for other people, pick olives for them. That way I could earn ten francs. And with the ten francs I could buy a kaleidoscope and watch the splinters of glass make patterns like stained glass in a church, see the colours of the rainbow."

What made you become a mercenary?

He wanted to express himself with his hands. But his hands were still manacled behind his back, and he could only kick the sand on the ground from time to time. Soon Maria reached the river with him. The water was very muddy, very murky, like the water in Venice. But the trees still cast their shadows on the water. Above the trees the sky, and in the sky clouds. He stooped down but couldn't get to the water. Maria cupped her hands together and scooped up some water. But the water had run away before it reached his lips.

"Do you know?" he said. "Last night, they alloted each of us soldiers ten francs. They called it an accident allowance. In a war, people are liable to have accidents. An accident is like a special assignment. It justifies an extra allowance. So they distributed an allowance of ten francs. Ten francs. It's just a piece of paper with a pattern on it. But I still hope I can buy a kaleidoscope with it."

He tried hard to stoop down. Maria looked at his face. He was very young, like a Corsican asphodel.

"How old are you?"

"Twenty."

She quickly scooped up some water and held it to his lips. But gunfire could be heard. It was coming from right behind them. Seven shots.

Maria looked up into the sky. She did not see his face.

"What's your name?"

"Maria," she replied. "What's yours?"

There was no reply.

Cross of Gallantry

Translated by Cecilia Tsim

Bhunah took out a handful of peanuts from his pocket and put them on my lap. Taking one for himself, he started shelling it and the skin fell in flakes all over me. Whenever Bhunah sees me sitting at my own door, he always comes over for a talk. He is like a younger brother to me, because, like my brother, he is also nine years old. I have no relatives in this city, and Bhunah always reminds me of my father, my mother, my young brother and sister. Ah, my father, what will he be doing now? Sitting on the rush mat in our house, forever making those leather drums. As for mother, she will probably have a big blanket wrapped round her, and she and my younger sister will be huddling beside the iron pan over the charcoal fire to keep themselves warm; for in my homeland, the weather usually gets cold around this time of the year. My younger brother is probably in the town square, sitting on the steps of the Stone Lion, trying to sell firewood, stacks of it all lined up beside him. I wonder if trade will be good today?

"Uncle Deehan, father says that you are going to slaughter the bull this year."

"I will do it if everybody says so."

"Not everyone can kill a bull."

"Many people do."

"My father can't!"

"He can."

"No, he can't! He said so himself. This was what he said. He said, "I can't do it, I am too old.' "

"He was being modest."

"How did you learn to do it?"

"Learn to do what?"

"Cut off the bull's head with one swing of the chopper." As he spoke, Bhunah raised his hand and cut through the air in one swift motion. He then took out some more peanuts from his trouser pocket, and put them on my lap again.

Bhunah likes to shell a peanut, throw it up in the air, and catch it in his open mouth. Sometimes he catches it, but sometimes he misses. And when he misses, he picks up the peanut (however covered it is with soil or dust), gives it a rub with his hands or brushes it across his trousers, and pops it into his mouth.

"Father said it will be a grand occasion."

"What will be a grand occasion?"

"When the bull's head falls at the first swing?"

"Oh, you're still on about killing the bull."

"It has to be absolutely spot on, doesn't it?"

"Yes."

"How did you learn to do it?"

"Practice."

"But how can you cut off a great big bull's head with just one swing?"

"It's a matter of practice."

"Uncle Deehan?"

"Yes?"

"Can you teach me how to cut off a bull's head?"

"You want to learn how to cut off a bull's head?"

"When I grow up I want to be like you."

"Good at cutting off a bull's head?"

"Yes, with just one swing of the sword."

"You wouldn't think like this if you were a bull."

"Why did you want to bring the bull into this?"

"If you were a bull, would you want to be slaughtered?"

"Uncle Deehan...."

"You still want to learn how to cut off a bull's head?"

"Will you teach me how?"

"Ask your father to teach you."

"No, I want to learn it from you."

"You will have to finish your homework first."

"That's a deal!"

"But you must do your homework first!"

"All right, I'm going back to do my homework right this minute!"

He ran off, leaving behind him a pile of peanut shells on the floor, and peanut skins littered all over me. On my lap were some peanuts still in their shells; beside the peanuts was my kukri. In my spare moments, sitting beneath the shade of the tree in front of my house, I like to take my kukri out and carefully inspect it, inch by inch. In fact there are not many inches to this kukri, but every inch of it is precious to me. This dagger is my only prized possession in this city; it is my only friend. It has been with me for many years; it has travelled with me from home to several countries. And now, in this city, it is all I have left. In my homeland, floods or droughts have caused havoc over the years. Food is short and life is very hard. That was why I joined the army so young.

In the old days, my father was a soldier too. But now he has grown old, and an old soldier cannot earn enough to support his family. So he gave me his kukri and got me into the army. The kukri which my father left me is very old. The patterns on the sheath—the rings of circles on the mouth of the sheath, the symmetrical hexagonal shapes around the middle portion, the grid of criss-crosses at the bottom—are all so faded as to be almost unrecognizable. The brass nail on the sheath has also long disappeared. But this is still a good dagger. Even in my homeland now, it is not easy to find another as good as this one. You can feel its weight when you hold it in your hands. And when you take it out of its sheath, its edge still radiates sharpness. Who would have expected such a good knife from its dark and tattered sheath? Towards the upper end of the dagger, near where the handle is, are etched the uneven marks of ringed corrosion. That strange dent looks like a bat in flight. The upper end of the dagger is tapered;

the middle is shaped like the neck of a vase; the lower end spreads out and bends sideways, curving outward, so that if I raise the dagger in my hand, it looks like a blazing torch, its flame blown sideways by the force of the wind. Sitting in the shade outside my house, I like to polish my dagger with care. I will never let it rust. I know this dagger so well. I can count the number of plum blossom nails on it, and the number of flowers the nails have formed themselves into. I can also remember the exquisite patterns carved on the face of the dagger, the dotted lines forming into leaves and the entwining creepers which give this tough blade an enduring charm. The two small knives that come with the sheath were already a little rusty when the dagger was given to me. But I have always kept them well oiled. And now, they are as bright and smooth as razors. This dagger will stay with me always. If I should return home in future, all I will take with me will be this one dagger which has followed me everywhere like a shadow.

Bhunah is only nine years old, but he is a strong and robust boy. He has thick black hair and a sun-tanned complexion typical of his Mongol blood. When he goes jogging with me, he can go half way up a mountain before pausing for breath. He could run further, but I won't let him, because jogging, like all other sports, has to be taken slowly and needs to be reinforced with regular, daily practice. No one should overdo it. When we jog, I deliberately slow down to keep him company. It makes him very happy, for he thinks he is running almost as fast as I am, although in fact he is still quite a lot slower. These days, he works really hard, and I can see that he is constantly improving. One day, he will be a very fast runner, better even than I am.

If my brother were with me now, he would be like Bhunah. He would jog up the mountains with me. In my spare time, I would take him on hikes; we would climb mountains and he would learn to tell the trees by their names, he would know how to star-gaze and predict the weather just by looking at the clouds. My brother would also grow up to be a strong young man. Bhunah is luckier than my brother; he can live with his parents here. And life here is definitely better than life at home. The question is whether, having grown up in this city, one should go back home? And if not, what could a Nepalese youth do in this alien, foreign city? I don't know the answer. As far as I know, everyone who has come here from my native land is a soldier. We first enlisted with the army and then we got posted with the garrison to different places. If I had not been a soldier, would I have come to this city? And if so, how? As a tourist? A student? On business? In this city I have not met anyone from my country who is an engineer, teacher, doctor or even a common clerk. Those who have come from the few big cities near my homeland are all standing guard in front of the shops. Only the very rich among my countrymen have been exceptions to this rule. What will Bhunah do, if he grows up here?

Maybe my brother is better off staying at home. During the Yerma Festival, he will sit against the wall with the sacrificial fruits and flowers all arranged in front of him in circles, and he will let his sisters make a red mark in the middle of his forehead. And they will say, "We plant thorns on the door of the God of Death, may our brother live to be a hundred years old." Many years ago, my elder sister planted such a red mark on my forehead and I became a strong and healthy lad. But my poor sister, she married a man in the country while she was very young. They now live in a thatched hut of clay and she toils in the fields with my brother-in-law. They do not even own an ox. I have seen my brother-in-law tilling the soil, using the plough that he made, while my sister, all in black and with a big plaid behind her, was holding a bamboo sieve with both her hands, scattering the seeds against the wind. She is only two years older than I am, but I feel she looks like a middle-aged woman.

A letter from father tells me there's been a flood in the country. The fields have been destroyed. They will have another poor harvest, and it will be difficult to make ends meet. People who live off the land live at the mercy of fate, they depend on the whims of the heavens above; they have no choice. They cannot move into their parents' place in the city. Everyone has his share of trouble to bear. If we were not poor, I would not have become a soldier.

Now my livelihood is not a problem any more. I do not need to worry about my meals and accommodation here. In fact my life in this city has actually turned out better than I expected. I send all my salary home, in the hope that my family will live a better life. Some day... but I don't want to think about the future. What sort of future does a solidier have? It is not like being in business; it is unlikely that I will earn enough money to buy a small house for my parents, younger brother and sister. The future? I'd rather leave the future to tomorrow.

"Uncle Deehan?"

"Yes."

"I didn't do badly today, did I?"

"You did better than last week."

"I practise every day."

"It's good if you can keep up your practice every day."

"I will try very hard."

"Good boy!"

"I want to run as fast as you."

"You will with more practice."

"Really?"

"Yes, really."

"I don't believe you. You are the fastest. You have to tell me why you are the only one who can run so fast."

"There are other fast runners too."

"Don't try to fool me, you are the fastest."

"Your father also runs very fast."

"Father said he really looks up to you, because you always come first at running uphill."

"That's because I always start ahead of the others."

"That's not true! I have seen you run before! Everybody starts together but in no time at all you've reached the top of the mountain. You move like lightning. Doesn't it exhaust you?"

"You get used to it after running for a while."

"Why am I out of breath after running less than half way up the mountain?"

"If you practise every day, you won't get out of breath."

"Is it all a matter of being able to make your breath last the distance?"

"With controlled breathing and more practice, you can run faster."

"Did you say my father can run very fast too?"

"He can run very fast and he can really run uphill."

"He said he is no match for you, do you know why?"

"Why?"

"He said it's because he likes to drink beer and drinking too much beer has slowed him down."

"It doesn't matter if you drink once in a while."

"Uncle Deehan, you stay away from beer and cigarettes because you want to keep fit and run fast, right?"

"No, I stay away from beer and cigarettes because I don't particularly like them. Also, I want to save up more money to send home."

"If I drink beer, will it slow me down too?"

"Kids should not be drinking beer."

"Uncle Deehan?"

"Yes."

"I've had enough rest now. Let's run again, all the way to the peak."

"All right, let's go."

The breeze is cool and refreshing. I know the hills and tracks around here well. Every day I make several trips up and down the mountain. I can almost recognize every single tree and the position of every stone. If I were not with Bhunah, I would have reached the peak a long time ago and would have made it back to the foot of the hill again by now. If I were not with Bhunah, I would have left this well-trodden path and would have headed up into the more difficult terrain. I would find my way through the thick scrub and the wild rocks. I really surprise myself sometimes. I am becoming more and more like a hunter. Only a hunter leaves the beaten track for the wilds, because he knows the most precious species are always hiding there, where few men venture.

"Uncle Deehan! Uncle Deehan!"

"Is that you, Bhunah?"

"Can I come in?"

"The door is not locked. Just give it a push and come in."

Bhunah pushed open the door and like a whirlwind he jumped in. I had on a long-sleeved shirt and was buttoning up one of the sleeves.

"Uncle Deehan, you've arrested a lot of people today."

"Yes, some."

"Father said he caught five altogether."

"He told you already?"

"He said you caught more, is that right?"

"I don't remember."

"Father said you caught seven all by yourself."

"It was a joint effort. Everybody had a hand in it."

"Are there many people trying to sneak in?"

"There are more these days."

"And they are difficult to catch?"

"It depends."

"They were saying that you did a great job this time. You arrested seven all by yourself. They said you're a brave soldier."

"Has your father come back?"

"Yes, he has. That's why I know you caught so many people today."

"This happens every day."

"Uncle Deehan, are your hurt?"

"It's nothing, it will be all right."

"There's blood on your hands."

"Oh, it's only red spirit."

"Why are you wearing a long-sleeved shirt? Quickly, let me have a look! Are you hurt like my father? Why don't you go to hospital? Father went. He was bandaged there and came back. He said those people were really fierce; some of them with knives even. Are you hurt? Show me.''

''It's nothing. My skin was slightly scratched. I've already put some red spirit on it. If I were really hurt, I would have gone to hospital, wouldn't I?''

''Did they really have knives?''

''Some of them did.''

''Did they use their knives on you?''

''Yes.''

''Did you fight them with your dagger?''

''No.''

''Why didn't you? You had a good dagger with you, didn't you?''

''There was no ill feeling between us.''

''But they stabbed you with their knives!''

''They did that because it was a matter of life and death for them.''

''But it was dangerous not to fight back with your knife!''

''I didn't want to hurt anyone.''

''But they could have hurt you, even killed you!''

''Danger is part of a soldier's life. You can get killed any minute.''

''But we are not at war.''

''It's exactly because we are not at war that I could not use my dagger.''

''They were difficult to catch?''

''Some more difficult than others.''

''Father said they were like foxes, very hard to catch.''

''But they're also like lambs, unable to really run away.''

''But unlike lambs, they had knives.''

''Many didn't have knives, many were still children; and there were some women too.''

''Father said the women didn't have knives, but they scratched with their nails and bit with their teeth. There are teeth marks on your hands. Were you bitten by them?"

"That's their only defence. They had no other way."

"Uncle Deehan, see, your arms have been scratched all over!"

"It's nothing. They will be all right in a few days."

My arms were not too seriously hurt. There were just scratch marks left by a woman's nails. After I had applied red spirit, they were all right. That woman was so skinny, but she had great strength. I found her hiding behind the rocks, curled up in the undergrowth. First she retreated backwards, until there was no more space for her to retreat into, and then she lay there like a wounded lamb. She knew that once we found her, there would be no hope of escape. She would be taken away and, after a while, she would be repatriated to wherever she had come from. I could see despair in her eyes. She was so disappointed and frightened. And then all of a sudden, she shot out from the undergrowth and got down on both her knees at a short distance from me. She bowed and kowtowed, started kowtowing to me non-stop. I did not understand her language, and I could not tell what she was actually saying. But what she wanted was quite clear. Similar incidents had happened to me many times before. They would kneel before me, amongst them young children, young women, old women, and even young men, and they would entreat with the plaintive look of despair and with tears all over their faces. All of a sudden, she reminded me of my poor sister back home. But I cannot be soft-hearted. I am a serviceman. I am a soldier. My duty is to catch illegal immigrants in these woods and hills. I am an enforcer of the law. I must carry out my responsibilities as a soldier, obey the orders of my superiors, arrest all who break the law, and help maintain law and order in this city.

If they run into me, they don't stand a chance. I know the terrain here. They are only intruders in a foreign land. None of them is my match when it comes to running, how can they get away? Even if they are not arrested by me, there is really no escape. There are troops everywhere, and like me, all the soldiers have undergone intensive training. They are good at combing the mountains and the rough country and they know the geography around here like their own back gardens. Ah, what good will it do them to kowtow to me?

Having decided what to do, I shot forward like an arrow, and in one movement I reached out and locked both her hands behind her back. There and then, she became like a beast in an arena; she scratched at me and bit my hands. But I know how to ward off such attacks and, one by one, I arrested them all.

The ones with knives are more difficult to handle. Of course, if I drew my dagger, they would not stand a chance against me. I can cut off a bull's head with one swing of the chopper. It would be child's play to cut off their heads. But I am always in control. I never allow myself to use the dagger. If I had used it, my kukri would be all covered with blood. I really have no grudge against these poor people. I assume that they too must have parents, brothers and sisters at home, that they are just a bunch of poor oppressed creatures driven to desperation by fate? And I am only a man who arrests, I am not a killer. But if they have knives with them, I have to handle them more carefully. That's why some troops arm themselves with assault rifles when they go on patrol. With rifles, of course, you've only got to aim at their faces, and these people have to give up.

Even without a rifle and without using my dagger, I still managed to arrest them one by one. I was not hurt. One girl made several scratches on my arms, and left a long mark with her nails, but these scars will heal. Today, I arrested seven illegal immigrants altogether. I suppose it was seven, because they said it was. Bhunah's father got five. He was slightly hurt. He must have returned home from hospital by now. In the barracks we were hailed as two brave soldiers.

I read my father's letter under the light. He said he had received the money I sent him, that they were all well at home and that I needn't worry about them. But the letter also said my brother-in-law had an accident while working in the fields. His hoe scraped one of his toes and he lost a lot of blood. When my sister saw what happened, she passed out. My brother-in-law became very weak and had a high temperature; it was not known whether the rust on the hoe would give him tetanus. They would write again if there was further news.

A lot of people came into my house just now. When they left, I did not close the door, and Bhunah popped his head in. I folded the letter properly and put it inside my pocket. Bhunah walked carefully into the house. He came in very slowly because he was holding a paper cup in his hand, and in the cup was a piping hot drink. Beside the cup he was holding, he also had a paper bag between his fingers.

"I'll treat you to a hot dog, Uncle Deehan."

"You bought these at this late hour?"

"There's hot chocolate in the cup, your favourite drink."

"Your pocket money will not go very far if you spend it like this."

"I can go without breakfast for a week, but I must come here to offer my congratulations."

"Where is your father?"

"He's at home, they are very noisy, drinking. I was here just now but there were so many people, so I did not come in. Luckily I had not bought the drinks and food first, or else they would have gone cold by now."

"Thanks for the chocolate and the hot dog."

"I salute you, Uncle Deehan. Congratulations on getting the Cross of Gallantry."

"Thank you, Bhunah."

"Oh, where's your Cross? Where have you put it?"

"In the drawer."

"Why don't you put it on display? Father certainly won't put his medal away in the drawer. He'll show it to everyone who comes inside the house. They are all very envious. This is a great honour. Everybody says so."

"Bhunah, have you finished today's homework?"

"All done, Uncle Deehan! Why don't you show me—your Cross of Gallantry? Is it the same as my father's?"

"The same."

"Father said the ceremony was very grand, was it?"

"Yes, very grand."

"Father said London is a big place, there are lots of pigeons in one of the squares, some Houses of Parliament by a river, and there's a big clock somewhere that strikes, and when it does the sound it makes is exactly like the sound of ferry bells here. Is it true?"

"Yes."

"Father said the parks over there are very big. Inside one of the parks, you can row boats, and there is a big church with stained glass, right?"

"Yes."

"Father said there were others who were awarded medals, and that there were different kinds of medals; the highest kind of medal is called the Victoria Cross. Is it true?"

"Yes."

"It is such an honour to be awarded a medal!"

"Bhunah, do you have to go to school tomorrow?"

"Yes I have to, but the house is packed full of people. I can go back a bit late. I cannot go to bed even if I go home now."

"This hot dog is very big. Shall we share it between us?"

"I bought it specially for you. We're celebrating!"

"We'll each have half, like brothers."

"Good, half each."

"Do you want some hot chocolate too?"

"We'll both have half?"

"Yes, each of us will have half."

"Uncle Deehan, it would be so nice if you were my real brother."

"Aren't you like my own brother now?"

"Uncle Deehan, I don't know why, I really admire you very much."

"Don't say such silly things."

"It's true, I really admire you, you are the fastest at running uphill, you can cut off the bull's head with one sweep of the chopper and now you have been awarded this medal."

"Your father is the one you should really admire."

"Uncle Deehan? When I grow up, will I be able to get a medal too?"

"All soldiers have the same chance of getting medals."

"When I grow up I want to be a brave solider, and I want a medal too."

"Bhunah, it's getting late now. You should be going to bed."

"I am so envious of people who have the Cross of Gallantry. Uncle Deehan, tell me, what are the people who have been awarded the Victoria Cross like? They must be great men, right? When I grow up, I shall be a good soldier, a brave soldier, and I want a medal."

"Bhunah, it is getting very late now, go home and sleep."

Finally, Bhunah went home. I locked the door, took out my father's letter and re-read it once more. I hope my brother-in-law will be all right. I opened the drawer and put the letter inside. On opening the drawer, I saw my Cross of Gallantry. It is a medal for bravery. I am a hero because in one day I arrested seven illegal immigrants. Bhunah said when he grew up he wanted to be a heroic soldier and he wanted the medal for bravery. Why does anyone want to be a soldier? If I had the choice, I would rather be a doctor or a teacher. Why can't I sell stamps over the counter in the Post Office, or be a driver in a public vehicle, or a carpenter making tables and chairs?

Today, I did not polish my kukri. I unfastened it from my waist and put it on the table. For how many more years will this dagger be with me? I don't know. Will I some day give this dagger to my child, just as my father handed it to me? I hope there will never be blood on this dagger. I even hope that this dagger will disintegrate with my body when I die. Or be used for nothing but chopping wood. My brother sells fire wood in the town square, sitting on the steps of the Stone Lion. Can the dagger be used to chop wood? I don't know. I have not tried. When it is Festival time, sister will put a red mark on my younger brother's forehead, saying as she does, "We plant all thorns on the doorsteps of the God of Death, may our brother live to be a hundred years old." Now, at Festival time, there is no one to put a red mark on my forehead. My sister is so skinny, standing there, thrashing husks against the wind in the open fields, dressed in black. How strange that the girl hidden behind the rocks was so like my sister! She made two blood-stained marks on my arms, one longer than the other, a vertical and a horizontal. They formed the sign of the cross.

Building a House:

Introducing Xi Xi

Stephen C. Soong

Forty years ago, Hong Kong was regarded as a cultural desert. It followed the classical laissez-faire model in cultural as in economic affairs: prosper or perish. And in the arts, most things perished. But in the past decade we have seen a great change. We now have most of the attributes of a cultured metropolis, and the government has gradually stepped in to subsidize them and ensure that they survive.

In literature we have as yet few things to pride ourselves on, and there is little the government can do to help. Even in countries with active and well-established literary scenes, writers cannot be trained by institutions. They develop through the careful and persistent nurturing of their talent. In Hong Kong the greatest single difficulty a writer has to confront is dialect: Cantonese is used in schools, at home, and in society, but the written literary language is based on Mandarin. The confusion created by this dual situation is obvious. A few brave individuals have tried to transcend the limitations of dialect literature by publishing their own magazines in Mandarin. But they have had limited success. It has been distressing to watch the local magazine *Poetry* cease publication after twelve years, and to learn that another literary journal, *Plain Leaves,* is in financial trouble. And yet, during the past ten years or so, Hong Kong has managed to produce a number

* *This introduction is adapted from a longer article which originally appeared in Chinese in* Ming Pao Monthly, *(Hong Kong), November 1985.*

of good new writers, despite the Cantonese dialect dominance. As Mandarin becomes more popular in Hong Kong, literature should prosper like the other arts.

One of these new writers is Xi Xi.

Her real name is Zhang Yan. She was born in Shanghai and moved to Hong Kong in 1950 with her family (who were originally from Guangdong province). Since graduating from the Grantham College of Education, she has worked as a primary school teacher.

In a short essay, Xi Xi has explained her choice of pen name. It has nothing to do with the sound (despite the bizarre romanized spelling, the words actually sound like the last two syllables of Assisi). It is just ''a picture, a pictograph''. Her account is so charming that I cannot resist quoting it in full:

> When I was young I used to love playing a game similar to hopscotch, which we called ''Building a House'' or ''Aeroplane Hopping''. First you draw a series of squares on the ground. Then you tie a string of paper clips into a knot and toss it into one of the squares and start hopping from one square to the next until you reach the square with the knot in it. Then you pick it up and hop your way back to where you started. When I played this game with a lot of other children, I always found it exciting; sometimes I played it alone, and felt very lonely. When I was in primary school, I played it all the time. Now that I am a teacher, I still play it with the children... The Chinese character 西 ''xi'' looks like a girl in a skirt, her two feet planted in a square. Put two of them side by side, and they are like two frames of a film, a girl in a skirt playing hopscotch in two squares.

From this, we can learn something of Xi Xi's attitude toward life: she is a person of childlike joy, a teacher who still enjoys playing games with her pupils. We can also see this particular game as a metaphor. The squares represent form or convention, and Xi Xi feels no sense of restriction; she can jump from one square to the next as she pleases. Or they represent the squares on the manuscript paper used by Chinese writers, the rules of the game Xi Xi the writer has learned to play and to break, though as she herself says, ''crawling from square to square'' (a standard metaphor for writing) is a more painful exercise than hopscotch.

In 1965, her first short story, ''Maria'', was published in the Hong Kong magazine, *Chinese Student Weekly*. The first time I read it, I was astonished and wondered how a publication designed mainly for local students and young writers, could have chosen a story based on such an outlandish subject. ''Maria'' won Xi Xi critical acclaim and her first literary prize. But like most of her subsequent writings which were published in *Plain Leaves,* it only reached a limited public, although she won a prestigious award in Taiwan in 1983 for her story, ''A Girl Like Me''. Do we have to translate the works of our own writers into English, and wait for Western critics to ''discover'' them, before we recognize them ourselves?

Two of the stories in this collection of translations merit a special note here: ''A Girl Like Me'' and ''The Cold''. ''A Girl Like Me'', written in the form of an extended monologue, is the haunting tale of a woman who works as a beautician in a funeral parlour. Her clear, rational voice reveals her belief that everything in life is predestined, that nothing can be changed. When her boyfriend brings her flowers, a traditional expression of love and a symbol of marriage, she sees this as a bad omen. Her heart is already broken. In the final line of the story, she says: ''He doesn't realize that in our line of business, flowers are a last goodbye.'' The words are spoken calmly as if nothing has happened; the effect is chilling.

On the surface, ''The Cold'' is also a love story of a middle-aged woman, told in the first person. But there the similarity ends. The protagonist of ''The Cold'' is already married, and leaves her husband to pursue a life of her own, while the beautician in ''A Girl Like Me'' submits to what she sees as her fate.

The greatest difference between these two stories, however, is not in their content but in the way they are presented. In ''A Girl Like Me'', Xi Xi incorporates her character's inner feelings and thoughts into the text, using flashbacks and narrative monologue to penetrate her character's psyche. In "The Cold", on the other hand, she quotes lines from well-known poems to express the protagonist's inner feelings. For example, when "Little Fish" delivers her doctor a wedding invitation, Xi Xi quotes from the classic *Book of Songs* (here given in Ezra Pound's translation):

Dark and clear,
Dark and clear,
So shall be the prince's fere.

Little Fish agrees to her betrothal, so it is suggested, mainly because her parents "suddenly discover" that she is already thirty-two:

The days and months hurried on, never delaying;
Springs and autumns sped by in endless alternation.

These lines are from another classic, the *Songs of the South.* There are altogether in the story twenty-six quotations from classical Chinese poetry: four from the *Songs of the South,* one from the great Tang poet Du Fu, three from Han dynasty ballads, and the rest from the *Book of Songs.* (Xi Xi has said that she likes the *Book of Songs* best.) These quotations are an effective means of presenting the protagonist's inner thoughts. The use of these famous old lines suggests that Little Fish is a person of education, someone who finds it hard to free herself from the constraints of tradition. Even at the first meeting between herself and Chu, her response is from the *Book of Songs:*

Now that I have seen my lord,
How can I any more be sad?

She does not attain her final liberation, in body and soul, until she goes swimming with her little brother; and then Xi Xi starts quoting modern rather than classical poetry:

I had not swum all winter. I had been feeling so tired, like a stranded fish, dry and dead.

And sooner or later your must share
In the making of grass.

After this, there are another eight carefully chosen quotations from the work of the contemporary Taiwan poet, Ya Xian. At the very end, when Little Fish decides to go and watch a soccer match, Xi Xi quotes again from Ya Xian:

Have you seen the showers wet the leaves, the grass?
Be grass and leaf
Be shower
As you will.

The shift to modern poetry in the quotations indicates a liberation from the constraint of the classics. From now on, she is no longer imprisoned in the past, but lives and finds her real self in the present. We know that she will marry Chu, but this is no longer important; she is now "free, a new person, full of life and joy".

In the Modern era, there have been a number of good Chinese short story writers. But there is not one novel comparable in scope and vision to the traditional Chinese masterpieces. Readers of this anthology may be curious to know whether Xi Xi is as successful a novelist as she is a story writer. There are some excellent scenes in her first novel *My City,* which describes Hong Kong life through the eyes of an uneducated, happy-go-lucky character, Ah Guo, an apprentice in the telephone company. Personally I find the long episode in which Ah Guo goes for a medical check-up one of the funniest things in Chinese fiction. But the structure of the book is very loose. Even though Xi Xi cut 100,000 words from the original 160,000 words of the newspaper serialization, somehow it still lacks the coherence of a novel in the proper sense.

In *Deer Hunt,* Xi Xi's second novel, she shows a more sophisticated craft in her successful manipulation of two parallel and intermingling story lines, in her employment of symbols, and in the way she alternates traditional and modern narrative techniques. Xi Xi has confessed that in writing this novel she was greatly influenced by the cinema.

Deer Hunt is in four "movements", like a symphony: "Autumn Hunt" (42 pages), "Moving Camp" (47 pages), "Country Feast" (40 pages), and "At Mulan Pasture" (37 pages).

The "music" itself has two motifs. The first is that of the Qing Emperor Qianlong, played in unison by the entire orchestra, inspiring the listener with a sense of classical grandeur and solemnity. The second motif is that of the hunter Ahmutai, gentle and lyrical, but full of modern modulation and dissonance. These two motifs are interwoven in an intricate pattern, and the whole is skilfully linked together by the overarching theme of the deer hunt.

Ahmutai's job is to lure the deer out into the open, and yet he himself is an innocent fawn, incapable of dealing with the complex outside world. He disguises himself as a deer, in his actions he is kind-hearted as a deer, and finally he loses his life like a deer. Qianlong, too, is a deer (as narrated by the "person with the strange eyes"), unaware that once he becomes the emperor he also becomes "a deer to be killed".

Deer Hunt is a successful modern novel blending elements of reality and fantasy: the Qianlong theme, with its juxtaposition of historical fact and imaginary inner monologue; the Ahmutai theme, pure product of the author's invention, transcending the traditional narrative limits of time and space. In this respect, *Deer Hunt* is highly innovative for a Chinese novel.

Xi Xi is very much a writer "Made in Hong Kong". The Hong Kong environment may not be very conducive to creative writing, but writers can at least pursue their goals without having to care too much about the pressures of tradition, or politics, or fads of one kind or another. Xi Xi regards children's tales, the cinema, and European and Latin American fiction as her major influences. She has read most of Andersen's and Wilde's tales, and her works are permeated with a childlike quality (is this perhaps also the product of her years of teaching in a primary school?). As a writer of film reviews, she was a great proponent of the "auteur" school, and this is evident in her emphasis on juxtaposition (montage) and "point of view" (camera angle).

Xi Xi grew up in a free society, a society with its own unique pattern of development. She has been able on the one hand to stand outside the main currents of contemporary Chinese literature; and on the other hand, although she received an English-style education, she was not unduly influenced by nineteenth-century European Romanticism or Realism. We find in her works neither sentimentalism nor any traces of Dickens or Balzac. She confesses instead to having been influenced by the Peruvian writer, Mario Vargas Llosa, and the Columbian writer, Gabriel Garcia Marquez. This is not to say that Xi Xi should be classed alongside these writers. Her writings are not transplants. They are thoroughly Chinese. It is hard to imagine "The Cold" having been originally written in English. In the first place, an English Little Fish would have immediately eloped with her lover. "Whether it was too late or not" would have seemed an absolutely absurd question to her. Then the poetry gives the story a very strongly Chinese flavour. In *Deer Hunt,* only a small portion of the subject-matter is taken from Chinese history. But the problems Xi Xi touches upon are those most Chinese are concerned with: the causes of political order and disorder, the relationship between ruler and people, etc. Her writing technique of course differs from that of her predecessors, but in the end Xi Xi is very much a Chinese writer.

Some Hong Kong readers may encounter these stories for the first time in English translation. Perhaps we should remember, after all, that when Hong Kong people travel abroad, they often discover that the souvenirs they buy to bring back home are inscribed: "Made in Hong Kong".

Translated by Kwok-kan Tam

A List of Xi Xi's Works

1. *My City* (fiction, Hong Kong, 1979)
2. *Cross Currents* (short stories and essays, Hong Kong, 1981)
3. *Stone Chimes* (poetry, Hong Kong, 1983)
4. *Deer Hunt* (fiction, Hong Kong, 1983)
5. *Spring Prospect* (short stories, Hong Kong, 1983)
6. *A Girl Like Me* (short stories selected from *Cross Currents* and *Spring Prospect,* Taiwan, 1984)
7. *Beard With A Face* (short stories, Taiwan, 1986)

Acknowledgement

Some of the lines of poetry in the story "The Cold" are reprinted with permission from the following:

1. *The Classic Anthology Defined by Confucius* by Ezra Pound (Faber and Faber, London 1955).
2. *The Book of Songs,* translated by Arthur Waley (Allen and Unwin, London 1937).
3. *Songs of the South: An Ancient Chinese Anthology,* translated by David Hawkes (Penguin Books, London 1985).